INNER MAGIC

The Power of Self-talk

Also by Sirshree

Spiritual Masterpieces - Self Realisation books for serious seekers
The Secret of Awakening
100% Karma: Learn the Art of Conscious Karma that Liberates
100% Meditation: Dip into the Stillness of Pure Awareness
You are Meditation: Discover Peace and Bliss Within
Essence of Devotion: From Devotee to Divinity
The Supreme Quest: Your search for the Truth ends there where you are
The Greatest Freedom: Discover the key to an Awakened Living
Secret of The Third Side of The Coin
Seek Forgiveness & be Free: Liberation from Karmic Bondage
Passwords to a Happy Life: The Art of Being Happy in all Situations

Self Help Treasures - Self Development books for success seekers
The Source of Health: The Key to Perfect Health Discovery
Inner Ninety Hidden Infinity: How to build your book of values
Inner 90 for Youth: The secret of reaching and staying at the peak of success
The Source for Youth: You have the power to change your life
Inner Magic: The Power of self-talk
The Power of Present: Experience the Joy of the Now
You are Not Lazy: A story of shifting from Laziness to Success
Freedom From Fear, Worry, Anger: How to be cool, calm and courageous
The Little Gita of Problem Solving: Gift of 18 Solutions to Any Problem

New Age Nuggets - Practical books on applied spirituality and self help
The Source: Power of Happy Thoughts
Secret of Happiness: Instant Happiness - Here and Now!
Help God to Help You: Whatever you do, do it with a smile
Ultimate Purpose of Success: Achieving Success in all five aspects of life
Celebrating Relationships: Bringing Love, Life, Laughter in Your Relations
Everything is a Game of Beliefs: Understanding is the Whole Thing
Detachment From Attachment: Gift of Freedom From Suffering
Emotional Freedom Through Spiritual Wisdom

Profound Parables - Fiction books containing profound truths
Beyond Life: Conversations on Life After Death
The One Above: What if God was your neighbour?
The Warrior's Mirror: The Path To Peace
Master of Siddhartha: Revealing the Truth of Life and After-life
Put Stress to Rest: Utilizing Stress to Make Progress
The Source @ Work: A Story of Inspiration from Jeeodee

Sirshree
Author of the bestseller *The Source*

innerMagic
The power of self-talk

Inner Magic
The Power of Self-Talk
By Sirshree Tejparkhi

Copyright © Tejgyan Global Foundation
All Rights Reserved 2008

Tejgyan Global Foundation is a charitable organization
with its headquarters in Pune, India.

Published by WOW Publishings Pvt. Ltd., India

First edition published in January 2008
Ninth Reprint in April 2019

Based on the Hindi book titled 'Swasamwad ka Jadu'

Copyrights are reserved with Tejgyan Global Foundation and publishing rights are vested exclusively with WOW Publishings Pvt. Ltd. This book is sold subject to the condition that it shall not by way of trade or otherwise, be lent, resold, hired out, or otherwise circulated without the publisher's prior written consent in any form of binding or cover other than that in which it is published and without a similar condition including this condition being imposed on the subsequent purchaser and without limiting the rights under copyright reserved above, no part of this publication may be reproduced, stored in or introduced into a retrieval system, or transmitted, in any form, or by any means, electronic, mechanical, photocopying, recording or otherwise, without the prior written permission of both the copyright owner and the above-mentioned publisher of this book. Any person who does any unauthorized act in relation to this publication may be liable to criminal prosecution and civil claims for damages.

Contents

How to get the most out of this book   07

Preface   09

SECTION I: THE TASTE OF SELF TALK

1. Listen Only To What Is Being Said; Say Only What You Should Say   17
2. Our Self-talk Shapes Our World   24
3. The Wonder Of Self-talk   34
4. Give Your Thoughts A Direction With Self-talk   38
5. Self-talk And Common Sense   42
6. Negative Self-talk - The Obstacle To A Supreme Life   46

SECTION II: HOW TO APPLY THE MAGIC OF SELF-TALK IN EVERY EVENT OF LIFE

7. Don't Be Hasty With Your Conclusions   57
8. The 'Ball' Of The Event And Self-talk   61
9. A Self-talk Message   65
10. Fix An Appropriate Price Tag To Every Incident   69

SECTION III: HOW TO APPLY THE MAGIC OF SELF-TALK IN VARIOUS FIELDS OF LIFE

11.	Self-talk And Complete Health	77
12.	How To Regain Your Remote Control	84
13.	How You Can Change The Entire World	90
14.	Self-talk And Body Language	96
15.	Get Rid Of Grief Resulting From Outflow Of Money	102
16.	Consider Your Work To Be Your Workout Regimen	105
17.	Learn To Finish Your Tasks Completely	109
18.	Captive Or Free	114

SECTION IV: HOW TO MAGIC OF SELF-TALK WORKS IN NATURE THROUGH SILENCE

19.	Self-talk Is Self-Reporting	123
20.	Convert Sadness into Happiness Through Self-talk	126
21.	How To Communicate With Nature In Silence	132

SECTION V: LEARN THE MAGIC OF SELF-TALK

22.	How To Carry Out Self-talk	141
23.	How To Benefit From A New Self-Affirmation Every Day	152
	Glossary	158

HOW TO GET THE MOST OUT OF THIS BOOK

1. Do read the preface of this book. Many important aspects have been explained in the preface which will help you to understand the contents given in the book in a better way.
2. To see miracles happening in your life because of self-talk and if you want to give your thoughts an appropriate direction, read Section V of this book without any delay.
3. To improve your relationships with all the people you interact, read chapters 13, 14 and 18 in Section III of this book immediately.
4. To converse with Nature or convert the feelings of unhappiness into happiness, and wish to report to the Universal Self within us with the means of self-talk, read Section IV of this book first.
5. Apply in your life the understanding given through the several stories, examples and phrases in the various chapters of this book. The mantras given in the stories will prove to be very effective in your life.

6. Check your self-talk while reading this book, and with the help of insights given in the book, change it accordingly. Doing so would help you to understand the effectiveness of self-talk instantly.

7. A list of 31 self-affirmations, one for each day of the month, is given at the end of Chapter 23 in Section V. Recite the given self-affirmation to yourself the entire day. Pick a new self-affirmation each day and work on it. Doing so, at the end of the month, you will have worked on 31 magical phrases.

8. From the list of self-affirmations given in this book, write down the ones which touch your heart and which you find effective, in your personal diary. Whenever possible, open your diary and read them as often as you can.

9. This is not a book but a workshop. The magic of the self-affirmations given in this book has already benefited millions of people and many more would continue to be benefited by it.

Preface

Those who desire to have the remote control of their life in their own hands will not refuse to learn the art of self-talk

Do you control yourself or do you let yourself be controlled by others? If you allow yourself to be controlled by others, it means that the remote control of your life is in somebody else's hand. When you are always connected to your heart (*Tejasthan*) and live a disciplined and happy life, then your remote control is in your own hands.

The remote control of man's life is divided into two (dual) parts. Living in duality is living in falsehood. The duality which exists in a false life includes:

- Respect – Disrespect
- Happiness – Sadness
- Joy – Misery
- Good – Bad
- Success – Failure
- Life – Death

These dual buttons exist on your remote control. If you have given the remote control of your life to somebody else, then you are living in the falsehood of duality. When you take charge of the remote control of your life and also have the right knowledge about how to operate it, then your life will be perfect. To live a perfect life the following five aspects have to be disciplined:

1. Mind: An ascetic mind like that of a yogi, a steady mind that can function unwaveringly in every situation.
2. Body: A healthy body; which when taken ill, gets down to heal and recuperate from any illness as quickly as possible. A body which has the power to fight any disease, a body filled with passion to live.
3. Intellect: A flexible intellect that allows space for new thoughts and ideas and is not rigidly stuck to old thinking and beliefs.
4. Consciousness: Awakened consciousness or supreme awareness, the brilliance of which will destroy all unconsciousness.
5. Aim: A complete aim, which gives a proper direction to the flow of the mind, body, intellect and Consciousness; where there is continuous flow of complete all-round progress.

Self-controlled life is a perfect life. The one who has understood the possibility of blossoming, opening up and freely playing the divine game of God (*leela*) that is going on upon the stage of this Earth, is ready to live a supreme life.

Man communicates with other people through language and with himself through silence. Conversation is the medium he uses in order to reach across to people. Prayer is the medium he uses to connect to God. He reaches within to the Self[1] through the practice of meditation. While engaging in these modes of contact, he is inherently engaged in constant self-verbalization or self-talk. Self- talk means talking to yourself within your mind.

---

[1]Self: the Universal Self, our true self, our original nature, Consciousness, Life, the Formless, the Witness, the Creator, God, the Almighty…

If a person happens to make an error in his choice of words while talking to another person, the people around him (such as parents, teachers, friends, well-wishers) immediately correct him by saying, "You should not talk in this manner!" However, when the same person is talking internally to himself, there is no one to correct him. As we grow up, we acquire the art of right conversation with the external world. However, we have never learnt the art of effective self-talk, due to two reasons:

1) We never felt the need to learn the art of self-talk.

2) We never came across anybody who has mastered this skill and is therefore able to guide us.

It is vital for us that self-talk takes place in the right way. For this, we need to first understand the importance of self-talk. It is only through self-talk that we can learn the technique of establishing contact with the fountain of eternal bliss within us. It is only through self-talk that we can improve our relationships and achieve all-round self-development. Upon understanding the significance and technique of self-talk, we can be totally liberated from misery. That is the magic we possess inside us. Those who aspire for a supreme life cannot afford to shy away from acquiring the art of self-talk.

We need to learn the grammar of self-talk. There are words that need to be avoided in self-talk. Not only do we need to identify such words, but we also have to get rid of them as though they were abusive. We avoid the use of abusive words in our conversations with others so as to maintain harmonious relationships. Likewise, we need to cast away negative thoughts in order to sustain harmony and a healthy relationship with ourselves.

We also need to understand the importance and use of punctuations in self-talk. We need to know where a comma should be put and where we should insert a full-stop (period), in self-talk. If we aspire to lead a perfect and complete life, we need to be ever-willing to learn the art of self-talk all over again. The successful mastery of this art ensures that we attain the goal. The goal of – eternal bliss, ample time at our disposal, a healthy life, unconditional love and self-satisfaction.

Let's waste no time and begin to learn how to do proof reading of our self-talk. This may seem to be difficult when you are required to focus as beginners, but very soon you will forget the mental fatigue when the results start speaking for themselves.

Just as one who learns music, unfailingly and consistently practices his art, similarly we need to apply ourselves regularly to understand and practice the art of right self-talk. We also need to regularly assess the nuances of our self-talk through contemplation.

Those who aspire for a perfect life are resolute about not going astray in external dealings as well as internal thought processes. They resolve to keep their feelings, thoughts, words and actions as orderly and beautiful as neat cursive handwriting. In our self-talk, our feelings, thoughts and actions should align in the same direction. This is the secret for leading life in the best possible way.

This book is your well-wisher. Well-wishers always wish the best for you. They always forewarn you about your mistakes so that you do not get entangled in any difficult situations arising out of your mistakes. A well-wisher not only advises you about your mistakes, but also provides you with appropriate solutions and suggestions so as to enable you to enjoy a happy and fulfilling life. This book acts as a guide showing you the direction where nobody outside can alert you. Is there any place where it is not possible for anybody to give you guidance? Of course! No one except you yourself can give direction to the self-talk that goes on in your mind. Helping you to do this successfully is the whole and sole purpose of this book.

The names of the people cited in the various examples in this book have been changed to avoid any inconveniences that could be caused to them. All the stories in this book have been written in a dialogue style so that apart from imparting knowledge, this book also sustains the reader's interest. After reading this book, do write and let us know how useful this book has been to you.

It is possible that we've never had a dialogue between us before this book. Hopefully we would have communicated with each other by the time you finish reading this book.

When the remote control of your life
is in your hands and you know
how the remote control is to be operated,
then your life will be perfect
and you will remain in the present.

SECTION I
THE TASTE OF SELF-TALK

The assumptions made by the mind
change the self-talk,
self-talk changes one's perspective,
perspective changes man
and man changes the world.

1
Listen Only To What Is Being Said; Say Only What You Should Say

It was evening time. A group of people were seated in a Satsang (spiritual group session). Many of them were asking a lot of questions. In the group, there was also a young lad about 25 years old, who was sitting quietly for a long time. However, his facial expression revealed that he had several questions brewing inside him. Finally, he raised his hand and asked a question.

"Sirshree, I have a question that has been disturbing me since a long time." Everybody turned around to look at him. "Often it so happens that while listening to your talks, I feel that I have understood whatever you have said. But, the next time when I hear the same talk which has been recorded on a cassette or CD, I realize that I had not heard the main point at all. While listening to you, I felt I have understood everything; however, in reality that was not the case. Why does this happen with me?" Hearing this, several people agreed that the same thing happens with them too.

Sirshree said, "When Sirshree is speaking to you, are you listening to Sirshree or are you listening to yourself?"

"What do you mean?!" all of them stated, "We are most definitely listening to you!"

"Okay! Let's take a small test" said Sirshree.

Everybody sat up carefully with an air of attention. There was pin-drop silence in the hall.

"Listen to this story. It's a tale of a city." Sirshree said. "In this city, there were buildings that were ten, twelve, fifteen and eighteen floors tall. Every day people would go about their daily grind to make a living. As in every city, there lived some good people and there lived some bad people. There were two buildings that stood opposite to each other, wherein one building had ten floors and the other building had twelve floors. In the twelve-storey building, there lived negative people like thieves, loafers and drunkards. In the ten-storey building, there lived people who did good deeds, who were positive thinkers and ever-ready to help others.

"One day both these buildings caught fire. People were running around screaming for help. There was total chaos. There was shrieking and commotion all around.

"Quickly call somebody to extinguish the fire!" Somebody in this din and roar yelled out.

"Oh! There are fifty people trapped inside the ten-storey building and five hundred people inside the twelve-storey building," a man said. Someone in the crowd called for an ambulance, which arrived promptly at the scene.

"Hurry! Quick! Put out the fire," a lady cried out.

"First, the fire in the ten-floor building should be put out," somebody yelled out. While someone else shouted, "First attend to the twelve-floor building..."

"Now there is a question for all of you: Which building's fire should be extinguished first?" Sirshree asked

On hearing this question, various emotions appeared on everybody's face. Some faces looked anxious while others looked unsettled, and some others showed mixed feelings.

Sirshree continued, "If it was easier to extinguish the fire of only one out of the two first, then which according to you would be the right choice – the ten-storey building or the twelve-storey building?"

Many answers started pouring in.

One of them stated, "There are five hundred people in the twelve-floor building. Therefore, it must be attended to first because more number of people are trapped in it. In the ten-floor building there are only fifty people."

"There are all good people in the ten-floor building. All of them are doing good deeds," a man about 50 years old, running his hand over his head, reasoned, "It is important to save these people."

Many of them agreed and one person said with conviction, "Instead of saving five hundred negative people, it is better to save the fifty good people…" The argument continued.

Sirshree reiterated, "We called the ambulance, then which building's fire should be put out first?"

Once again there was a buzz and some opined that it should be the ten-floor building, while others insisted it should be the twelve-floor building.

Sirshree with a smile on his face said, "But an *ambulance* does not extinguish fire."

And a stunned silence fell in the crowd… then people started laughing and clapping.

"In the story it was told that the ambulance was called, not the fire-brigade!"

As soon as Sirshree explained this once again, everybody broke into laughter all over again.

"What does it mean? Even after hearing the word 'ambulance', we did not take in the meaning of what it stands for."

A different type of gleam could be seen in everybody's eyes.

"How do we listen? We listen with our self-talk going on in the background; we listen with whatever is imprinted in our memories. We assume that this is what must have been told and believing so, we get on with our talk, discussing and debating. We simply waste our time or lose the depth of the subject matter. What we *want* to hear is exactly what we hear. What we *want* to say is exactly what we say, whenever we get an opportunity to say something."

On hearing this, everybody was compelled to contemplate upon the fact that we hear what we want to hear; and that if we want to say something, then we keep searching for a logical reason to put forth our point during a conversation. We constantly search for an excuse to speak whatever we like to speak. There is a very big reason behind this: The dialogue within the mind – Self-Verbalization or Self-Talk. If we understand how this self-talk works, then we will also be able to understand how our mind functions. We can also perceive how we listen and what things we speak to ourselves.

After knowing this secret, we get the insight that *whatever we hear is not necessarily the truth and that we must speak to others and with ourselves only what ought to be spoken.*

Many a time we do not hear exactly what is it that the other person is saying and without even listening to him we form our opinion. That is why the real problem is left aside and we keep working in a different direction; how then will the problem be solved? Having known this secret, let us now understand the secret of dialogue.

The secret of dialogue

Suppose you ask someone, that in his entire life span till now, who is the person with whom he has had maximum conversation? On hearing this question he would most likely begin to think, 'In my childhood did I speak the most with my mother?' Then the answer he might get would be, 'No! In fact, it was my mother who used to talk the most with me. I wanted to speak to father many-a-time, however I was not able to gather enough courage to speak to him. Conversation with him would take place only at those times when it was necessary to obtain his signature on the School Report Card. Most of the time spent with my brothers and sisters was wasted in quarrelling. It would so happen that for days together I would not speak with them due to those fights.'

After that, the question arising in his mind may be, 'Is it with my friends that I have had a lot of conversation?' Once again the answer would be, 'No! There have been many days when I did not meet or contact my friends.' 'Is it that I spoke a lot with my teachers?' Pat would be the reply, 'I could hardly dare to speak to my teachers! With them, it was only listening. In those days, I had to think ten times even before asking a question!'

'Then which person is it with whom I have spoken the most? Is it with my wife…? With her, I have seldom had a chance to speak at all. She is the one who does most of the talking. The children barely meet me, so when do I ever get to talk with them? They are much more interested in the television or internet than in me. Speaking with my boss usually means uttering the words "Yes, yes" softly and repeatedly. Or for a change, saying very sweetly, "Right!"

'I can't think of any other person with whom I have had the maximum conversation!' And… suddenly this man gets a jolt. 'Hey…! Right now, who am I talking to? Maybe this is the one with whom I talk the most. I talk the most with *myself!* I keep talking to myself, perhaps all the time. Be it day or night, morning or evening, every moment I keep speaking to myself.'

If we look back at our life, we will find that the extent of conversations we have had with others is no match to that which we have had with ourselves. Till today, whatever free time we had, has been spent talking to ourselves. Rather, the dialogue begins automatically within us, and we are unable to stop it even if we wish to.

Be it any topic, the series of thoughts begins within us; irrespective of whether the given topic is related to us or not. When we are alone, thoughts constantly appear in our mind. When we are conversing with others, then too the stream of thoughts does not stop. Contemplating on this, we realize, 'Whether alone or in a crowd, at both places, the dialogue taking place the most is with **myself**. Many times or perhaps every time, I talk with two people at the same time. One is the person in front of me, and the other is myself.'

We often spend a lot of time thinking, 'What would my friends think about me? What would my relatives think about me?' But we hardly reflect on, 'What would I think about myself or what do I really think about myself?' and actually thinking on this is most essential. **More important than what people think about us is what we think about ourselves.** And, in fact, this is much easier and natural because we listen to ourselves the most. There are many aspects within us that reveal to us about ourselves.

Just as we start thinking something or the other about every person we come across, likewise, we keep thinking a lot many things about ourselves too. We narrate to ourselves what we believe and what assumptions we make as we go through various events in our life. We listen to our inner conversation and begin to lead our life based on it. The dialogues we have with others can possibly be curtailed. We may choose to not meet people we dislike, we may choose to not listen to unwanted topics, but how will it be possible to run away from our own self? How do we put a stop to the constant chatter that goes on inside us?

We cannot run away from ourselves; so we are left with no choice but to listen to our internal conversation. When listening to songs, we have the choice of either listening to them or not. If such a choice was made available, there would be some who would choose not to listen. But if it is decided to listen, then anyone would obviously like to choose a good song. People would mostly like to listen to those songs which motivate them. We listen to songs for pleasure. Sometimes songs also inspire us, but that is an added benefit. If we treat our life to be a song, we can be inspired to such an extent that we can accomplish our goal. Come, having known the secret of Listening and Dialogue, let us now understand the secret of joy and sorrow.

I am free of criticism,
I have given up complaining and blaming.

2
Our Self-talk Shapes Our World

Everyone wants to know how their miseries can be brought to an end and how their difficulties in life can be overcome.

However, should amassing joys and eradicating sorrows be the objective of life? No, this should not be the objective.

The main objective in man's life should be to understand how joys and sorrows get created in the first place. If one understands how joys and sorrows are created then our life will be successful because by understanding the actual reason behind sorrow, we will begin to come out of the cycle of joy and sorrow. Subsequently only those actions will be performed through us that are a source of eternal bliss.

So come, let us understand the factors due to which joy and sorrow are created in our life.

This story is about a man whose name was Sukhram. This story was narrated to many people. It is now being narrated to you.

The aim of Sukhram's life was to possess all the best things that life could offer and to have all the pleasures that existed in the world. With this intention he started his business. A few years later he became a very big businessman. He achieved great success in his business and made a lot of money. He built several mansions and bought a lot of articles to adorn his lavish mansions.

He had all kinds of luxuries, yet he always felt, 'I have everything; but I have not found that happiness, that feeling of joy, which will last forever. This happiness that I have today may not be there tomorrow. It is ephemeral.'

In spite of acquiring all possible luxuries, Sukhram was feeling somewhat miserable inside. He used to get very annoyed and feel distressed if anybody behaved against his wishes.

A thought troubled Sukhram all the time, 'What is it that I should attain that would permanently liberate me from misery? How can I remain in joy all the time?'

As these thoughts became stronger, one day he arrived at a firm decision – "Let me search for such happiness that will be never-ending such that my entire life will be filled with bliss."

With this thought he sold off his entire business, houses and luxuries. He sold off everything he had, and with all the money he got, he bought diamonds. The diamonds were just twenty to twenty-five and could fit into a small pouch. He tied the pouch containing those diamonds and tucked it securely around his waist, and set out on his journey.

He travelled to various places. Whichever place he went, Sukhram asked people, "Can anybody over here

tell me where I can find such joy and happiness, on the attainment of which, I will not be sad about anything in my life? Such that my life thereafter will be filled only with contentment and bliss?"

Sukhram's voyage took him from place to place but there was nobody who could answer his question. He sojourned across many countries in vain and began feeling disillusioned. Negative thoughts started creeping up in his mind and he thought, 'Perhaps there is no such thing as permanent happiness. The very nature of life is such that sometimes there will be joy and sometimes sorrow. There will always be ups and downs. The journey of life will follow this beaten path. It is not possible that one will find only happiness in life.'

One day he met a hermit. The hermit told him, "Sukhram, life is like the two sides of a coin. After joy, sorrow has to follow." He further stated, "After sorrow, joy has to follow; this is Nature's law." The hermit spoke with such certainty that Sukhram had no choice but to agree.

However, deep within him he had a feeling, 'This cannot be possible; there must be some way by which all miseries will end.'

His inner voice kept forcing him to seek for it.

Then one day somebody told him, "Towards the North, next to the mountains, there is a small village. There lives a saint (an ascetic). Perhaps he will be able to give you the answer to your question."

Sukhram thought, 'Well, as I have already travelled all over, why not try there too?' So he strode towards that village. When he reached the village and observed the villagers who lived there, he did not feel that there could be some saint staying there, who would be able to reveal to him the intricacies of how joy and sorrow are created and how one could be liberated from sorrow. Nevertheless, he asked the villagers,

"Does any knowledgeable saint live here?"

"Yes, but why do you ask?"

"I have come from very far just to meet him," Sukhram replied earnestly.

"Next to that mountain you will find the saint sitting there," the villagers informed him.

Sukhram started walking towards the mountain that the villagers had pointed out. After quite a walk he reached the foot of the mountain. He saw the saint seated under a tree. As soon as the saint saw that a person was walking up to him, he called out from afar and asked, "Why have you come here?"

Sukhram stopped in his tracks and greeting the saint with folded hands replied, "I have spent several years searching for real happiness but until now I haven't found such happiness." Sukhram's voice seemed to come from the depths of his heart. "Can you please tell me how I can achieve such kind of happiness that will never end so that sorrow cannot enter my life? Is it possible for you to give me such joy, such bliss?"

The saint smiled softly and mischievously asked him, "If I do give you such happiness, then what would you give me in return?"

On hearing this question Sukhram approached the saint. He pulled out the pouch containing the diamonds, and held it in his palm. "Sir, this pouch contains diamonds that are worth millions. All the wealth that I have earned in my life is here in this pouch." He stated with a look that showed both politeness and solemnity. "I can hand over all this wealth to you."

Saying so, Sukhram placed the pouch in front of the saint. The saint cast his glance affectionately towards the pouch, then looked at Sukhram, then looked back at the pouch, and before Sukhram could understand anything, the saint swiftly got up, grabbed the pouch and started running as fast as he could.

For some moments Sukhram could not figure out what had transpired. Then suddenly he comprehended the situation and realized that the saint had taken flight along with his diamonds worth millions.

"Catch him! Catch him! This man is running away with my entire wealth! He appears to be a saint but is actually a robber, a scoundrel..."

Screaming loudly, Sukhram started chasing the saint. The saint was running so speedily that it was impossible to catch him. Sukhram was trying to keep up as fast as his legs could carry him but every moment the distance between the two was widening. The saint ran all around the village. Sukhram was hot at his heels. The entire village folk were watching them. They were bewildered at this sight.

Sprinting, the saint returned at the foot of the mountain and stood hiding behind a tree. Sukhram in pursuit also reached that place. His mind was filled with profound pain at this unfortunate turn of events and he stood there gasping for breath. At that moment the saint threw the pouch containing diamonds in front of him.

Sukhram quickly picked up the pouch to check whether all the diamonds were there or not.

On seeing all his diamonds intact, Sukhram was delighted. The saint standing behind the tree called out to him and asked, "Are you happy now?"

"Yes," Sukhram said with a sigh of relief.

On hearing this answer, the saint appeared in front of him.

Sukhram looked at him. The saint's face was lit with laughter, joy as well as the answer to Sukhram's question, which Sukhram could now so very clearly decipher.

As soon as he read the answer on the saint's face, Sukhram's facial expressions changed. A different kind of glow appeared on his face.

He looked at the pouch containing the diamonds and then looked at the saint. He did this several times. Suddenly he dropped the pouch on the ground, went towards the saint and fell at his feet in reverence. Now there was a look of gratitude in Sukhram's eyes.

The question that arises here is that when Sukhram was asked, "Are you happy now?" why did he reply that he was happy?

Thereafter, why did he drop off the pouch of diamonds, which he was so eager to possess just a few moments ago and was anxiously chasing all around the village?

And then why did he go and touch the saint's feet?

What understanding did Sukhram gain from this incident, due to which he renounced his entire life's earnings and surrendered before the saint?

When this question was asked to people during a discourse, various answers were offered.

"Due to the running and chasing Sukhram realized what is happiness?" an old man inquired.

"When we lose something, then we realize its value," stated another.

"Till the time the diamonds were with Sukhram, he did not realize their true worth and was oblivious to any happiness," a man around 40 replied in a matter-of-fact manner. "As soon as the diamonds were taken away from him he realized the loss as those diamonds were very expensive. When he regained them he felt happy because of having found them again."

"When the pouch was taken away from him, Sukhram felt that he was the poorest man in the world. Due to this thought, he was frantically chasing the saint to recover his wealth. When he got back the pouch he became very happy because he felt he had become the richest man in the world. It is for this reason that he might have become so happy." After hearing such a reply from a young man, several people nodded their heads in approval.

"He took a lot of effort in running and chasing; that is the reason why he became happier," said another.

"All this is correct, but if that is so, then what is the insight he gained, due to which he fell at the saint's feet in reverence?" Sirshree questioned.

On hearing this, many faces appeared contemplative.

"The saint demonstrated that happiness is not outside, it is within us," a lady answered. "The saint illustrated that happiness is not in wealth or diamonds; all these are just an illusion (maya). Real happiness is inside us."

"Okay, this is also correct. But where within you is happiness?" Sirshree asked.

Now everybody started thinking.

Sirshree continued, "What understanding emerged in Sukhram due to which he gave up the diamonds? This is something to be reflected upon. To shed some more light on this point, we shall take up another small story, with the help of which you may be able to grasp the core secret. Then we shall see what is it in both the stories that can explain why Sukhram renounced his wealth and fell at the saint's feet.

"There was a businessman who used to run a small enterprise. One day he received a letter at his residence. The back cover of the envelope indicated that it had been sent from a city in the state of Karnataka. As soon as he saw that the letter was from Karnataka, his face turned red with rage. He threw the letter away in a corner because the letter had come from Karnataka.

"His wife, from whom he was seeking a divorce, lived there. His wife would send him letters several times and would often use abusive words. She would always ask for money and trouble him with such demands. He used to be forced into sending her money. Hence, on seeing this letter, he got furious thinking, 'She must have written this letter for money again! She must have spent all the cash I sent her last time.'

"After about ten minutes he retrieved the letter from the corner, tore open the envelope and removed the letter thinking, 'Let's see what is it that she has demanded this time.' He started reading the letter, and as he continued reading, the anger on his face began to fade and gave way to joy. In fact, he was totally exhilarated because that letter was sent by a company in Karnataka placing a big purchase order in the name of his firm. On seeing such a huge purchase order he got crazy with excitement.

"Several thoughts popped up in his mind such as, 'Now I will buy a big house… I will purchase a fancy car… I shall have all the best things in the world…' With such thoughts his happiness knew no bounds.

"If we look back, this was the very letter which had provoked him and filled him with fury on thinking that it was from his wife. The second time when he picked up the letter and read it, he was thrilled. Now the question here is, why did this happen?

"In the same way when Sukhram had the pouch containing the diamonds, he had neither joy nor sorrow. But when the pouch was stolen, he was in grief. When the pouch was returned to him, he became happy. What was the underlying reason in these two stories? How are joy and sorrow created in our life? This needs to be contemplated upon deeply.

All the people listening to these stories had a big question mark on their face thinking, 'How is it that the two stories are pointing towards the same thing? The two stories appear to be quite different!'

Sirshree cleared the doubts by stating, "It is true that the two stories are different, in which the incidents that took place created joy and sorrow."

"This means that when Sukhram had the diamonds, he was not happy. When he lost them and then got them back, he realized the value of the diamonds," a man who had been silent all this time stated. "He felt grief, then felt happy, so the value of that wealth, that which was already so valuable, increased manifold. In the same manner, in the second story, the businessman initially was anguished thinking that it was his wife's letter, but when he found that it was a purchase order, he became doubly happy because that happiness came after agony."

"It is right, if joy comes after grief, it creates more happiness. But what is the underlying factor hidden in these two stories? What is the cause of sorrow and joy in our lives?" Sirshree asked.

"Sirshree, I have understood!" The look on the face of the person who stated this was that of hitting upon a huge discovery. With his index finger dancing about, he exclaimed, "It is right, right it is! Now I have understood how joy and sorrow are created. They are created by our thoughts! You have always said that joy or sorrow is not caused by any event, it is caused by the thoughts that commence inside our mind due to that event."

Sirshree smiled, "Absolutely correct! No incident is joyous or sorrowful in itself. **It is the self-talk that begins at the time of the incident which brings about joy and sorrow.** The incident of the loss of the pouch did not create sorrow; it was the thought 'my pouch is lost' that created sorrow. In the same way, the thought 'I have got my pouch back' produced happiness. Self-talk means the thoughts that keep running in our mind, which is the reason behind joy and sorrow. The self-talk, 'this is my wife's letter' generated sorrow. And the self-talk, 'this is not a letter but a huge purchase order that will change my life', generated joy.

"This is the truth, which applies to everyone in this world. Joy and sorrow begins with our self-talk. **We create our world with our self-talk. Likewise, we create either heaven or hell for us and begin living in it.** The more this secret unfolds before you, the more you will be amazed, and this amazement will go on mounting. At the end, you will come to know that **until *you* do not wish to become unhappy, nobody can make you unhappy.**"

When you were reading the two stories and listening to the answers given by people, what was the self-talk going on within you? What were your answers? Do not consider any answer to be the final answer as yet; you have just started reading this book. The magic of self-talk has not yet been revealed to you. So be ready for new surprises in the next chapter of this book. 'Nobody can make you unhappy' – enlighten yourself with this truth.

The adversity that does not terminate me makes me tougher.

3
The Wonder Of Self-talk

There were two friends named Mangesh and Pankaj. Pankaj had borrowed ten thousand rupees from Mangesh. After some days Mangesh started asking for his money from Pankaj. Pankaj now tried to evade him all the time.

One day, all of a sudden Mangesh suffered a massive heart attack. The doctor examined him and pronounced him dead. When Mangesh's wife heard the doctor's verdict, she was shocked and she fainted. When Mangesh's son heard about his father's death, tears began to flow from his eyes. When Mangesh's servant heard about his master's death, he was disturbed. The atmosphere in the house was filled with grief and worry.

At the time when Mangesh died, Mangesh's neighbour was reading the newspaper. He called out to his wife and informed her, "Our neighbour Mangesh has had a massive heart attack, and he is no more." After giving this news to his wife, he continued reading his newspaper. The news of Mangesh's death did not have much effect on him.

"Who knows what can happen nowadays," the neighbour's wife remarked. "There is no certainty about man's life." Saying so, she turned back to her kitchen chores.

On hearing the news of Mangesh's demise, the self-talk that started in Pankaj's mind was, "I had borrowed ten thousand rupees from Mangesh, and this fact was known only by the two of us; no one else is aware of this. Now that Mangesh is no more, I do not have to return the money. Good for me! Now with this money I will buy a new smart phone. How nice it will be to watch videos and chat with my friends on WhatsApp!" Pankaj thus began fantasizing and was lost in his dream world.

From this example, you can understand that a single event had different effects on different people. Why did this happen? On Mangesh's demise, self-talk along different lines commenced in each individual's mind. The self-talk took either negative, positive or neutral form in each one. Every self-talk initiated the cycle of joy and sorrow in each individual.

While reading this example, what is the self-talk going on inside you? Stop reading this book for two minutes and listen to your self-talk. Do you now agree that the assumptions of the mind change the self-talk, self-talk changes one's perspective, perspective changes man and man changes the world? If you don't, read this example further.

If death is bad, Mangesh's death should have generated sorrow in all, however, this did not happen. If an incident makes one happy, it should make everybody happy, or if it makes one sad, it should make everybody sad. But it never happens in this manner because everybody looks at the incident through his or her own perspective and begins with their own self-talk. This self-talk could be either positive or negative. During the occurrence of self-talk, the person himself is not aware of it. However, the self-talk leaves its impact and the person finds himself swinging in joy or sorrow. When he snaps out of it and his awareness awakens, his self-talk changes. Right from childhood, a person's mind gets programmed into a specific structure and pattern, due to which his self-talk originates. By breaking this internal structure or pattern, one can attain a supreme life.

Hearing about the demise of Mangesh, all his family started mourning, but after some time, unexpectedly, Mangesh's heartbeat revived.

When Mangesh's wife noticed this, she fainted in happiness. When Mangesh's son heard that his father was alive, tears started flowing from his eyes. However, this time the tears were that of joy.

Mangesh's servant, who was feeling very disturbed, now regained his composure and got back to his work.

When Mangesh's neighbour heard of this news, he called out to his wife and said, "Did you hear what happened? Our neighbour Mangesh has not died; he is alive and awake." Saying so, he once again immersed himself into his newspaper. "You just can't trust doctors now-a-days," the neighbour's wife shook her head. "They pronounce a living person as dead." Saying so, she returned to her kitchen chores.

When Pankaj received the news that Mangesh was still alive, he felt dejected. The self-talk that began in his mind was, "I will now have to return his money. Why did this happen? I cannot buy the smart phone now. My dreams of buying that smart phone are shattered..." With such self-talk, Pankaj felt morose because he would now have to pay back the borrowed money.

Having gone through this example, you would now have understood that happiness, 'bright' happiness (*Tej-anand*, real inner happiness, which is unremitting eternal bliss), is not due to external events. In the example above, if the reason of sorrow was Mangesh then everybody should have felt sad, however it is not so. In this incident, one felt happy while the other felt sad. If the reason for sorrow was

Mangesh then who was the reason for joy? What this means is that Mangesh was not the reason for sorrow; the reason for sorrow was something else. The reason for sorrow is the self-talk that is going on within everybody. This self-talk can happen in ignorance and unawareness or can also happen in full awareness and with complete knowledge. There is perpetual self-talk taking place inside us, due to which any incident that occurs becomes either happy or sad. When you understand this secret, you will have known the principle for attaining liberation from sorrow. Working on this principle consistently will help you to achieve a supreme life.

Incidents take place in your life all the time. Certain incidents affect you whereas certain other incidents do not have any effect on you. During those incidents or after those incidents have occurred, the 'contrast mind' begins its commentary, giving you live reviews of those episodes. It is from here that the entire drama of joy and sorrow begins. (The contrast mind or outer mind has been described in detail in further chapters and also in the glossary).

From the above example, you have understood how essential it is for our contrast mind to receive training and knowledge. Only after receiving this training and knowledge will its wrong commentary end (the miseries that arise due to self-talk). When the contrast mind's commentary is terminated, the intuitive mind will get more opportunity to work. (The intuitive or instinctive or inner mind is described in more detail in the further chapters and in the glossary). The intuitive mind is always ready to perform every task in a beautiful manner. It is due to the dominance of the contrast mind that the intuitive mind is unable to perform much. The contrast mind has its own agenda (casting doubts, being judgemental, creating ego, provoking distrust), due to which a person lives in misery instead of living life in the best way possible.

4
Give Your Thoughts A Direction With Self-talk

The mind of every individual, that indulges in self-talk every single moment, is the root cause of all unhappiness. You watch your mind involved in self-talk day and night, from morning to bedtime, as you rise, sit, eat, drink, walk or work. If the contrast mind is restored to health, i.e. if its self-talk turns positive, then everything else will become alright. Just like by watering the roots of a plant, the whole plant grows and blossoms, similarly, by nurturing the root which represents the mind, the body (epitomized as the plant) will become healthy and begin to blossom. This is possible with positive self-talk.

The habit of the contrast mind is to perpetually compare things, judge them up against preconceived notions and indulge in negative self-talk. It always keeps prattling in every incident saying, "What has happened is good... That shouldn't have happened, that is bad... Now I am feeling miserable... Now I am feeling happy..." In this manner the contrast mind applies labels to every event. It is constantly engaged in self-talk. It is always influenced by transient gain and loss.

The mind feels happy at one moment and sad the next. An example of a teacher and students is illustrated below to help understand how man's contrast mind indulges in incorrect self-talk and thereby continuously tangles and untangles itself from the cycle of good and bad.

"Children! We all are going for a picnic tomorrow," the teacher announced and the classroom exploded with sounds of excited squeals and clapping of hands.

"Wow! It's going to be great fun. That's cool!" Many such sounds could be heard in the classroom. Just then, the teacher lifted up her hand and the commotion receded.

"Every student will have to pay eight hundred rupees for the picnic," informed the teacher and a pin-drop silence fell in the class.

"Oh no! The amount is too much," spoke a girl softly. Her voice was tinged with unhappiness.

"I shall not be able to go for the picnic, this is bad. I wish I had more money," some children voiced their discontent.

"It will cost eight hundred if we travel by plane," the teacher stated with a wide grin. "But if we travel by bus, each student will have to pay two hundred. Therefore, we will travel by bus." The class broke out into a loud applause.

"Yes! We will go by bus. We can afford two hundred rupees. We will also be able to do some shopping there. This is a good opportunity!"

"But I have just come to know that all the picnic spots are already over-booked."

"Oh no! This is terrible. Why do we face such hindrances in our program?"

"But we have found a spot at Juhu Beach."

"Oh, great! Wow! We will eat, sing and make merry. Everything is okay now."

"We will be served sago (sabudana) during the picnic."

"Eeks! Do we have to eat tasteless food that is consumed during fasts? Then what kind of picnic is it going to be?!"

"Only those who are observing a fast will be served sago. The rest will be served biryani and curry."

"Yeah! Great! That's my favourite dish. It's going to be real fun."

"The Principal will also accompany us."

"Oh! There goes our fun…"

"But he will be there only to see us off."

"Great! It is alright then. We will be free to sing and dance and make merry."

From this conversation, you understood how man's contrast mind turns happy or sad during a single incident, due to self-talk. Now understand the exact reason why the state of the mind keeps changing all the time. The mind has the habit of labelling each thing as 'good' or 'bad'. It is this mind, which sticks labels to everything, that is called as the contrast mind. The contrast mind attaches either a white or a black tail-tag to every event. **The self-talk of the contrast mind inside man is the root cause of sorrow.** You need to work upon your self-talk. Man's difficulty lies within him. So does the solution.

Man is interested in knowing the self-talk that goes on in others' minds, he would want to read others' thoughts. But by wishing so, he would not be able to attain a supreme life. What man most essentially needs is to know the self-talk going on within himself, and to change it intentionally. When we do not give our thoughts a proper direction, they become the cause of problems. Give your thoughts the right direction in complete awareness with the help of your self-talk. When your thoughts get the right direction, you will experience that your happiness has not been lost; it has always been there with you.

The following analogy will make this fact clear. There was a woman who was carrying her child tucked up behind her back. She was anxiously asking all the people around, "Have you seen my child?"

"No, we have not seen your child," everybody told her. For a long time the woman continued to frantically search for her child. Finally, at dusk, she asked a person one last time in despair whether he had seen her child.

The person casually asked her, "You are not talking about the child you are carrying on your back, are you?" That was when the woman realized that all the while her child was tucked onto her back. Then a thought popped up into her mind, 'I asked so many people, but no one told me that my child was with me on my back. Surely some of them would have noticed this child!'

People may have felt that the woman was searching for some other child; how could it be possible that she was looking out for the child she had tied behind her own back? That was the reason why people did not inform her about that child.

This is exactly what is happening with man. Man is himself carrying the solution to his sorrows, he is himself carrying his happiness, and yet he is asking everybody, "Where can I find happiness? How will my life become the best? Where do I find real happiness?"

Now you sit down and write down all those self-dialogues that would help you to give your thoughts a proper direction, which would help you to enhance time, love, health, wealth and contentment in your life. Whenever you find time, read through these self-dialogues repeatedly. Your Supreme Life has begun...

5
Self-talk And Common Sense

Another trait that is required to experience the magic of self-talk is 'common sense'. It is very important to possess common sense but hard to find nowadays. A boy told his friend, "It is good that I was not born in a Gujarati family." His friend was surprised and asked him, "Why do you say so?" The boy replied, "Because I do not know the Gujarati language." This gives you an idea of his level of common sense. It is common sense that if he were born in a Gujarati family, he would know the Gujarati language.

How to get desired results through self-talk

Once a man sat on a donkey with a cane in his hand. On one end of the cane, he tied a banana and suspended it in front of the donkey's face. When the donkey saw the banana, it moved forward in the hope of grabbing it. However, as much as the donkey moved forward, the banana remained ahead of it because the man who was dangling the banana was seated on the donkey. The more the donkey paced ahead, the banana too with the same pace remained ahead. Due to the absence of common sense, no matter how hard the donkey tries, it does not succeed. Man too, many a time, works hard but does not attain the fruit of his labour. What man needs to do is to use his common sense as much as possible. If success is hard to come by, he should have a self-talk and tell himself, "What are the three major reasons of this work not yielding any results? I need to write them down in my diary. Next time, what is it that I should do differently so as to achieve good results? What is it that I have learnt from the mistakes I have made? I should write them down." In this manner, your self-talk and writing things down would help you achieve the desired outputs of all your inputs.

Self-talk is the reason for happiness and grief

What is the goal of Supreme Life? The goal is to achieve Bright happiness, eternal happiness. After all, that is what each one of us is seeking. Even the person running after money is in fact searching for this happiness. It is in quest for this happiness that people indulge in liquor, drugs and gambling too.

Whenever people gather in a group, they start gossiping and speaking ill of others. By doing so, they derive false happiness and seem to like it very much. People should have the common sense to know that if they criticize others behind their backs, this action rebounds into their life in the form of misfortune. Use your common sense and stay away from such gossip. If you want to talk behind somebody's back, why not talk about his or her good qualities? It is better to say a word of appreciation rather than criticize anybody. This way you shall spread goodness among people.

When two or more ladies meet, they invariably start criticizing others because they too derive pleasure in picking on others. Actually they are yearning for that inner happiness but since they are not aware of the true inner happiness, they try to satisfy themselves with false happiness.

Like the donkey that kept pursuing the banana, a money-minded person keeps chasing money without using his common sense. He keeps saying to himself that if he goes just a little further, he will achieve his desire – just a little more money and he will get what he wants (fulfilment). Man always thinks that if he can turn his one lakh into two lakhs, or one crore into two crore rupees, then he will be happy. But it is not so. His entire life he keeps chasing like the donkey and happiness always remains a few paces ahead of him. You need to snap out of this dumb tangle.

To come out of this tangle you need to use your common sense. Understand that **every individual is in search of happiness alone, and that happiness is present right within us.** All you need is to have the art of recognizing it. With understanding of the truth you need to become so receptive that as soon as anybody imparts the truth (supreme truth) to you, you would instantly experience the truth and the eternal bliss.

If the actual intention behind every action of man is to experience happiness, then how can this happiness be attained? Is it really so easy to attain such happiness? Man is troubled by his thoughts several times in a single day. One thought makes him cheerful while the next one makes him miserable. Thus, your 'self-talk' becomes the reason for both, your joy and sorrow. How this happens can be understood by the following example.

Two friends meet each other after one has completed an examination. The dialogue between them will help you gain an insight regarding when do thoughts (self-talk) create joy and when do they create grief.

First Friend: The examinations are finally over today.

Second Friend: Wow! That's good news.

First Friend: But today's examination was on a very difficult subject.

Second Friend: Tch! Tch!

First Friend: However, we could cheat a lot in the examination hall.

Second Friend: Wow! Great!

First Friend: But I was caught cheating.

Second Friend: Tch! Tch!

First Friend: But the teacher let me off.

Second Friend: Great!

First Friend: But then my father came to know about it.

Second Friend: Tch! Tch!

First Friend: But, my mother saved me.

Second Friend: That's great!

First Friend: However, dad told me that I will not be allowed to spend my vacation at my cousins' place.

Second Friend: Tch! Tch!

First Friend: But luckily, this time my cousins are coming over to visit us.

Second Friend: Wow! That's great.

It is clear from these dialogues, how our talk changes constantly with every sentence. Our self-talk makes us feel happy or sad. Negative talk generates unhappiness. Positive talk brings joy. And talk of the Supreme Truth creates Bright Happiness. In reality, where is happiness? Is it in thoughts? Or is it at the source of thoughts (the Self), at which we need to stabilize? Supreme Life unveils this secret.

I am glorious. I never lose my glory. I have given up worrying.

6
Negative Self-talk - The Obstacle To A Supreme Life

What self-talk did God have with himself, due to which he decided to create this universe? What would have been His self-talk after creating this universe, which led to the creation of Supreme Life? Come, let us understand this with the help of words and a hypothesis.

After creating the universe, God first created 'time' and 'space'. But He did not derive as much satisfaction as He expected after creating the universe. So He created one more entity – 'living being'. To enable living beings to carry out their activities smoothly, He placed an intuitive/instinctive mind in each of them.

Instinctive Mind

A human being's mind is a single, undivided entity but to understand it comprehensively, we need to give it different names. At this moment, let us consider the mind to have two different names – 'instinctive mind' and 'contrast mind'. Let us understand their mode of functioning and their significance.

Instinctive mind is that mind which conducts every activity in a straightforward and appropriate manner, as per its understanding. You too would have experienced that whenever you perform some task with your instinctive mind, you never know how time flies by.

Think about the time when you were involved in a creative job. You would have spent five hours absorbed in it without even noticing the time. When you later looked at the watch, you might have exclaimed, "It's so surprising! Five hours have slipped by and I did not even realize it! How did this happen?"

When God planted the instinctive mind into the human being it became a novel or unique form of life. However, again, God did not feel as elated as He would have liked to. He was faced with the question, 'How can supreme happiness be derived?' So He felt the need to add something more to the human being due to which He would be able to experience the joy of his creation (universe).

After having created the instinctive mind, God came up with an innovative creation. In today's parlance, this creation is termed as the 'contrast mind'. Contrast mind signifies that mind which splits everything into two and persistently compares and evaluates things with their pros and cons. It splits things, thereby creating duality such as good-bad, black-white, joy-sorrow, greater sorrow-lesser sorrow, knowledge-ignorance, success-failure, etc. You must have seen the contrast button on your television set. Next to this button there is a picture of a small circle, where half the portion of the circle is painted white and the other half is painted black (◐). Likewise, the contrast mind also divides everything into two and that is the reason why it is called as the contrast mind.

When you perform any task, your contrast mind begins its commentary – "How long will this take…? How will it happen…? This work is so boring… should I do that other task first…? Why do I have to do all the work…? No matter how hard I slog, the credit will go to someone else; then why work at all…?" The contrast mind gives you a live commentary (giving details of the actions of people around you). You have heard the live commentary going on during a cricket match. The people listening to it get caught up into its grip and sway to its tune. If the commentary is positive according to them, they jump up and down in excitement. If the commentary is negative, they get so annoyed that they smash things around. These reactions of people arise out of the self-talk that goes on inside them. The contrast mind incessantly keeps on chattering. Even at this moment, as you are reading this book, there is something or the other that your contrast mind is intermittently commenting upon. Some dialogue must be certainly taking place in your mind. This commentary of the contrast mind depends on its knowledge or ignorance, what it has heard and the information it has. When God created this marvel of a contrast mind, He felt jubilant. Why?

The contrast mind instantly labels every event as 'good' or 'bad'. It labels according to its preconceived notions. E.g. If a person hears about the birth of a baby boy, his contrast mind comments, "Very good, it's a boy!" (This belief is mostly prevalent in India). And if it is a baby girl, it remarks, "That's unfortunate!" The contrast mind decides everything in advance. If somebody praises you, you would thank him. And if someone speaks foul of you, you would curse him. The contrast mind has already decided what response it shall give to specific incidents. In this way, the contrast mind keeps commenting inside you and evokes automatic, thoughtless responses from you. If you do not remain alert, the contrast mind causes sorrow, instead of happiness for which God had created the contrast mind. In order to derive happiness, God experimented by planting the contrast mind in various different beings. This is just an example meant for vividly illustrating some points. Do not consider it to have happened for real. It is just a way of encouraging you to understand and contemplate. Through this example you need to try and understand the following – 'Who am I?' 'What exactly is the life that is present inside me?' 'What is the real obstacle in life?' 'What is it that I need to realize in order to live the rest of my life in the best way possible?'

The donkey and the contrast mind

God had initially created living beings, before creating the contrast mind. It is from living beings that life blossomed. When there was no contrast mind in living beings, life was being led in a simple and pleasant manner, however, God was not satisfied. To attain more happiness, God wanted to devise something amazing. So He created the contrast mind, the human mind.

God had several beings before Him into which He could place the contrast mind. He wondered, 'In which being should I place the contrast mind?' Just then, He saw a donkey pass by. It was wandering happily in the jungle. God inserted the contrast mind into the donkey to see what kind of self-talk occurred inside it. The donkey's self-talk took place on these lines: 'The whole world's burden is laden on me. Why me? Have I taken up the contract of carrying everyone's load?' This kind of self-talk made the donkey very unhappy. God was amused at the donkey's level of intelligence but He did not experience that happiness which He so desired. He asked the donkey, "How do you like your contrast mind?" The donkey replied, "The contrast mind gives me only unhappiness. It does not give me any different kind of happiness." Hence, God removed the contrast mind from the donkey and then went about looking for some other creature.

The deer and the contrast mind

After a while, God sighted a deer. Moments ago, the deer had managed to save itself from the jaws of a tiger after a difficult scuttle. The deer had then spotted a green pasture and had begun to eat the grass. God saw the deer and placed the contrast mind inside it. Immediately, the self-talk of the contrast mind began – 'A little while ago a tiger was chasing me. What if it had killed me? What kind of a world has God created? In this jungle there are so many evil animals roaming around, waiting to kill poor animals like me! In this jungle there are some criminal animals and some innocent animals. All the criminals should be eliminated from the jungle. If God has created such monsters, why did He make me so timid? Why am I such a coward? If the tiger comes back tomorrow, what will I do? At this moment, I cannot even relish this green grass. What is going to happen?...'

Such self-talk made the deer feel very worried and the non-stop acrobatics of thoughts began inside it. God then asked the deer, "Apart from these thoughts, do you feel anything different on receiving the contrast mind?" The deer replied in the negative. God then removed the contrast mind from the deer and went looking for some other being.

The dog and the contrast mind

When God was not pleased by introducing the contrast mind into the donkey and the deer, He put it into the dog and waited to see what kind of self-talk occurred in the dog's mind.

As soon as the contrast mind entered the dog, the self-talk that began inside it was: 'I am such a good animal; I wag my tail on meeting anybody. I admire everybody but what I get in return is only rebuke. Why does this happen with me only? I am good to all, I am faithful to all, yet everyone chides me and drives me away. The dog from the other neighborhood comes and barks at me in my own territory. Now if that dog returns I will teach him a lesson...' The prattle of the contrast mind in the dog went on. God thought, 'The contrast mind is doing a fairly good job in the dog. However, I am not pleased to the extent I had expected when I created this game (*leela*). Let me experiment on some other beings.'

The ant and the contrast mind

After the dog, God placed the contrast mind into a tiny little ant. The ant was happily engrossed in scurrying about but when the contrast mind entered it, it started grumbling: 'God is so partial! How has He made this world! He has made me so tiny and the other creatures so big. God shouldn't have treated me in this manner. It would have been so nice if I had wings. Today people just trample me under their feet. The entire day I just roam here and there; it gets so boring!' God realized that there was no exceptional or distinct effect the contrast mind had on the ant.

The monkey and the contrast mind

God then inserted the contrast mind into the monkey and began to watch its effects. A few moments ago, the monkey was jumping around from branch to branch. As soon as the contrast mind entered it, it started muttering: 'Why did God make me so ugly? I wish I had beautiful eyes and a chiselled nose. When will I become handsome and successful?'

You know that many people are not able to accept the way they look. They are always unhappy about their appearance. They too keep thinking in the same manner as the monkey – 'How I wish I had sharp features… and good height… and lesser weight…' People are simply not able to accept their body as it is. The contrast mind always keeps on rejecting something or the other. People cannot accept their body favourably and cannot even hide their feelings of disappointment.

The monkey was also thinking on these lines. God did derive some satisfaction over the work of the contrast mind in the monkey, however, it was no match to the happiness He found by placing the contrast mind in the human being.

Human being and the contrast mind

Finally, God introduced the contrast mind into the human being. Immediately, man's complaints started flowing in thousands. The contrast mind began its self-talk: 'Why did God create so much disparity? He has made some people poor and some people rich. He shouldn't have done this. One man is a criminal and the other is a victim. One person likes one thing and the other person likes something else. Some people have a melodious voice while others are cacophonous. There shouldn't have been such differences. Why is there night after day? Why is there darkness after sunlight? Why are there illnesses and worries? Why do lust, anger, cravings and greed exist? Why does man have to earn money to feed himself?...' Man thus has never-ending complaints. He lives an unsatisfied life indeed. He constantly thinks about what should be there and what not.

Just try to imagine, if everyone in the world were rich, how would the world be? If nobody was poor, would you have servants and attendants in your house? How would your office and home function? Who would build houses and who would cultivate crops?

Thus, God experimented with placing the contrast mind in various beings but He was not satisfied. When He placed the contrast mind in man, He attained true happiness. He experienced self-realization in man by utilizing the contrast mind. This experience would not have been possible without the contrast mind. After experiencing this state, the contrast mind was permanently placed in human beings. As long as man does not understand the enigma of the contrast mind, he will continue being unhappy due to erroneous self-talk.

God created the contrast mind to forget himself (conceal and keep the Self as a secret). He created Science to propel man towards progress. And He created 'Bright' Truth (*Tejgyan*, knowledge of the Supreme Truth) so as to enable Himself to be a witness to this divine game through man.

Ignorance of the contrast mind

The contrast mind does not understand that '**all the activities in the world are running in a planned, orchestrated and automatic manner.**' The contrast mind is ignorant of nature's way of working, and therefore it always indulges in negative self-talk. When the contrast mind comes to realize nature's secret, it surrenders itself in awe, appreciation and devotion. When the surrendered mind engages in self-talk, waves of happiness and love surge in the body. This self-talk is no less than the great Upanishads (Holy Scriptures which contain the content of the dialogue that transpires between the spiritual master and the disciples). It is for annihilating the contrast mind that all spiritual paths and meditation techniques had been invented. It is for annihilating the contrast mind that you are being given the understanding of living life the supreme way.

Man's contrast mind in its ignorance desires that everybody should have a melodious voice, everybody should be rich and everybody should be handsome. But one should try and understand that only if there are some people with shrill voices around, the ones having a melodious voice will stand out and be appreciated. If everyone in the world had the voice of Kishore Kumar or Lata Mangeshkar (famous singers of India), nobody would listen to anybody. This way, under the influence of the contrast mind, you would have eliminated a wonderful thing like music from this world. Music is a delightful component of this world and due to the way of thinking of the contrast mind you would have destroyed it.

If God were to be influenced by the contrast mind and make everybody rich, tall, fair, good-looking, strong, intelligent and honest, imagine what would happen! You wouldn't find this world worthy of living. Man thinks that when all is well, everyone is beautiful, everybody has a melodious voice, then there would be happiness. But, when you comprehend the reality, you will not like that kind of life.

When the contrast mind manifested in man, all the things that God wished for began happening. God saw that the enjoyment for which he had created the contrast mind has begun. The contrast mind will initially become strong and then the day it crashes down; it will be the happiest day. It is necessary that the contrast mind be made stout initially, so that when it is eventually knocked down, it will lead to immense happiness. It is like when a person who has been away from home for a long time is overjoyed upon returning home and says, "There is no better place than home anywhere in the world." But all the while when he was at home before going away, he did not realize its value. The joy and peace that he felt upon returning home after a long time made him realize its worth!

I am ready to transcend my old boundaries and lead a new life. I am now freely expressing my qualities.

SECTION II
HOW TO APPLY THE MAGIC OF SELF-TALK IN EVERY EVENT OF LIFE

To give proper direction
to your thoughts
and to give an appropriate response
to every incident,
changing your self-talk
can be the best approach.

7

Don't Be Hasty With Your Conclusions

The solution to a problem lies within the problem itself. If self-talk is the problem, its solution also lies in it. Let us understand through a tale how self-talk can keep you balanced or neutral in joy and sorrow. Else even a trivial mishap leaves you distressed.

A long time ago, in a village, there lived a man with his son. He was a very old man. His name was Shunya baba. Shunya baba would always be in a neutral state, i.e. he remained balanced at all times. No event could disturb his mental balance. He was well adept at 'remaining in zero or nothingness (*shunya*)'.

He possessed a horse. This tale belongs to those times when people's wealth was judged by the number of horses they owned. More the number of horses, more wealthy was a person considered.

One day it so happened that his horse strayed away. Perhaps it got lost. Everybody started searching for it but it could not be found even after a long hunt. The villagers came to see Shunya baba. They told him, "Shunya baba, this is a sad event. What has happened is very bad. You had only one horse and now it has gone away. It is a big loss." But Shunya baba was neutral, 'in zero'. His face looked peaceful and there was suggestion of a smile on his face. He calmly said, **"How can you so hastily proclaim that what happened is bad and has resulted in a loss?"** The villagers were astonished at this reply. They said, "You mean to say that what happened is not bad?! Your horse is gone which means your wealth is gone. Is this not a big loss?" saying so, the villagers left.

A week passed by after this incident. It so happened that Shunya baba's horse, which had lost itself in the jungle, returned. During its venture into the jungle, the horse had befriended several other horses. When it returned, eight of them also accompanied it. Now Shunya baba had nine horses in all. This news spread in the village. Soon all the villagers gathered at Shunya baba's place to have a look at the horses. Now everybody started praising Shunya baba. "Shunya baba, this is such a great event! You are rich now, this is good for you. Your fortunes have opened up, you are so lucky, your wealth has increased nine fold."

Again Shunya baba was absolutely placid. He had the same smile, he was 'in zero'. Remaining in that neutral state, he said, **"How can you so hastily proclaim that my fortunes have opened up, and that what has happened is good?"** The people exclaimed, "If this is not good, then what is it? Your wealth has increased and you ask us how can we hastily say that it is good!" saying so, the villagers went away.

The horses that had come from the jungle were wild. It was necessary to train those wild horses. Shunya baba's son was training the horses, and during one stint, he fell off a horse and had a bad accident. He broke his leg and became disabled. He was in a lot of grief. Shunya baba was busy nursing his son, applying medicine and bandage on the broken leg. The villagers once again came to meet them and said, "Shunya baba, what has happened is very bad." The villagers were feeling sad. The only son of Shunya baba was lying there totally incapacitated. He needed crutches to walk around. This was during the times when one had to toil hard and earn his own bread. In those times there were no offices where you could go, sit and work to earn money. There were no such facilities. The villagers said, "Shunya baba, this is such a sad incident, very bad! It's your misfortune, your only son is handicapped." In spite of this, Shunya baba was calm. With the same calmness and tenderness, he said, **"How can you so hastily proclaim that what has happened is bad and that it is a very unhappy incident?"** Seeing Shunya baba in a neutral state even in such a situation, people were baffled as though they were struck by lightning. Some people mumbled amongst themselves, "This old man seems to have lost his sanity. He is unable to bear the pain of seeing his son in such a state and that's why he is talking like this." Shunya baba understood their talk, yet he was 'in zero'. People were saying, "If not bad, then what is it? Your son is handicapped." Shunya baba was still neutral. Calmly he tended to his son. The villagers left.

A few months later, the province in which the village lied was attacked by the king of a neighbouring province. As soon as war broke out, all the young men in the province were ordered to join the army. Shunya baba's son, being disabled, was exempted from joining the army. There was a bloody war. The war was finally won, however, all the youths from the village died in the war. When the news spread in the village, all the villagers came to Shunya baba and said, "Shunya baba, what you said was true. No matter how your son is, crippled or handicapped, but he is still with you. We no longer have our sons with us. Our sons are no more, but your son is alive." Some people started to cry and told Shunya baba, "It is so good that your son is with you." Shunya baba was serene all this time. With the same serenity, looking into nothingness, he said, **"How can we so hastily proclaim that what has happened is good or bad?"**

In this story, Shunya baba tells us that immediately after any incident has taken place, our self-talk begins, "This is good… this is bad…

this is better… this is worse…" We have to remember this message given by Shunya baba. Whenever a good or bad event occurs, before our run-of-the-mill self-talk begins, another kind of self-talk should be done by us: "Whatever the incident may be, we must not hastily proclaim it to be good or bad. Let the day go by. Only after some time passes by, we will be able to decide whether the incident was good or bad."

Try and recall all those events that have happened in your life in the past. What do you feel about them now? Recall those incidents which, five or six years ago, you had found to be very bad and negative. What do you feel thinking about them now? You would probably feel that those incidents were not as bad or as negative, as you had perceived them to be at that time. This means that whenever an incident occurs, our self-talk instantly starts along the lines of: "This is bad… this is good… this is better… this is worse…" Henceforth, we shall always keep Shunya baba's neutral message in mind. Whatever may be the incident, we will not label it as good or bad at once. We have to go towards 'zero', stay near 'zero', stay in 'zero' and always keep Shunya baba's message with us. After every event we have to just say, **"How can we hastily proclaim what has happened is good or what has happened is bad?"**

I know that life cares about me.

8
The 'Ball' Of The Event And Self-talk

There are some people whose self-talk proliferates endlessly after a couple of good occurrences that take place in their life. They just cannot come out of their fancy drooling. It may be only a small success which they have achieved, but they indulge in so much self-talk that they ignore the success that has come into their hands at present.

This is exactly what happened to a boy called Chunky. Although Chunky was a hardworking lad, he would spend all his time cooking up fantasies. One day in his college it was declared that there would be selections for putting together the best football team of the college. This team would be sent to play for an esteemed club. Chunky immediately enrolled for the selections. As soon as he put forward his name, he started building castles in the air... "If the ball comes to me in this direction, I will kick it in this manner... I shall shoot a goal like Beckham... I shall dribble in style..."

His friends were watching his condition precariously. One of his friends, a considerate man, offered him advice, "Chunky, stop your fantasies. Yes, you may definitely plan your moves and shots, but if you keep escalating your fantasies in this manner, the ball may not come to you at all. Say to yourself, 'First let the ball come to me, then I shall think how to kick it.'"

Chunky could not understand what his friend was telling him. He turned up for the selections on the stipulated day. Everybody had a drill and displayed their prowess. The team was selected. Chunky was not on the list. He was upset. Depressing thoughts cropped up in his mind. His friend said, "Look! If you had listened to me and stopped cooking up fantasies, you would have been able to focus on your practice and you would have definitely been selected."

The friend then said, "Come on now, it's okay. Pull up your socks and practice with me." Chunky started practicing with him. After two days of hard practice, Chunky began playing very well.

His friend thought, "Wow, he can really play!"

He called Chunky and told him, "Chunky, I have some good news for you. One of our players is not able to join the team for some reasons. We have to pick someone else in his place. I have three names in front of me, you included. Come to the ground tomorrow at eleven."

Chunky duly reached the ground. The two others were also present. Their coach was to choose one boy among them. He put them through a test. Chunky demonstrated his skills well. "We have selected Chunky," announced the coach after the drill. Chunky was overjoyed.

The coach then said, "In case of injuries, we shall have two backups in Ramesh and Raju."

Elated, Chunky went and sat beside the ground. His day-dreaming began. He could see the ground choc-a-block in his imagination. In his mind's eye, he saw the stadium filled to capacity and making a lot of noise. Chunky saw himself playing to the full house, kicking the ball in style and earning applause from the crowd.

He was imagining that somebody gave him a nice pass and he kicked it into the goal. The crowd was delirious and chanted his name. Chunky then imagined that they had won the game and the trophy was in his hands. He heard someone calling his name and then other players were trying to grab the trophy from his hands. It could be clearly seen on Chunky's face that he was lost in his own world. The self-talk within him was on at full throttle. Chunky felt that some players were shaking him up. He thought that they were trying to get a hand on the trophy. Chunky rudely pushed aside the person next to him.

In reality, the person who Chunky pushed aside was the coach himself. The coach fell down on the ground. Chunky did not even realize that he had pushed the coach. He was still in his dreams. The coach left angrily and struck out Chunky's name from the list. Chunky's friend ran up to him, shook him hard and asked, "Chunky! Why did you push the coach? He has expelled you from the team." Hearing these words Chunky snapped out of his dreams.

His friend advised him to remember his words throughout his life – "In any incident, tell yourself, '**First let the ball come to me, then I will kick.**' Do not start indulging in fantasies in advance."

We too have to do the same when either a good incident or a worrisome thought occurs. 'Will I miss the train? Will I miss the bus? Will I get good food in this hotel?' When such questions, 'yes or no' questions, 'will be or will not be' questions appear in your mind, tell yourself, "First let the ball come to me, then I shall see." How you kick the ball i.e. how you respond to the situation, should be seen when you actually face the event. You get sucked in the whirlpool of thoughts before anything happens. Of course, it does not mean that you should not take precautionary measures.

You should definitely take precautions. Do decide in advance what you should do if you miss the bus. But if your thoughts keep on running endlessly, or negative self-talk begins, say to yourself, "First let the ball come to me, then I shall think how to kick it." If you leave home and start thinking that you may miss the bus, say to yourself, "If not this bus, I'll take some other one. I'll decide once I get to the bus-stop." If you leave for work and get a feeling that the boss will scowl at you today, say to yourself, "First let the ball come to me, then I shall see how to kick it." Right now, do not think of whether you will pass the ball or kick it into the goal. Do not get entangled in such hollow thoughts. Take precautions, but if thoughts engulf you or negative self-talk begins, say to yourself, "**First let the ball come to me, then I shall see.**"

I am a part of God's creative opus. I therefore take part in creative and inventive ventures.

9
A Self-talk Message

There once lived a businessman called Rameshlal. He had worked hard all his life. He had accumulated a lot of wealth and he had also learnt the art of living life. Whenever he found time, he always wanted to share a lot many things with his two sons. Sometimes his sons would listen to him and sometimes not. When he grew old, Rameshlal decided to have a discussion with his sons. The elder one was Sumesh and the younger one was Deepak.

One day Rameshlal called them together and said, "I am growing old, I don't know how long I will live.

While I am still alive, I wish to divide my entire wealth and hand it over to both of you."

He then divided his wealth into two equal portions. He gave one portion to his elder son Sumesh and one portion to his younger son Deepak. He told them, "You have to take your share and start living for yourself. From here on, you depend on yourself." Both his sons obeyed him and started working with their portions.

After a few days Rameshlal passed away. His sons rushed home on receiving the news. They were very sad. Together they arranged for the funeral and last rites. After performing all the rites, Sumesh and Deepak returned home. They were cleaning the bed on which their father used to sleep. Under the mattress, they found a small wooden box. They opened the box. There were two rings placed in it. Sumesh and Deepak were surprised. One ring was of gold and the other was made of silver. The silver ring looked quite ordinary. The golden ring had a valuable diamond fixed on it. Sumesh said to his younger brother, "This is our father's last token." Deepak nodded in agreement.

"Dividing this diamond into two would not be right," said Sumesh. He further added, "How should we share this? Let us do one thing, you keep one ring and I'll keep the other." Deepak agreed to it.

"You keep the silver ring, I shall keep the golden ring," Sumesh said decidedly. Deepak thought that this was not the moment to argue, so he accepted his brother's verdict.

The elder son Sumesh took the golden ring studded with a diamond and left. Deepak took the silver ring. For many days Deepak kept wondering, 'My father was such a knowledgeable and intelligent man. He divided all his wealth into two but why did he keep the expensive diamond ring to himself? More surprisingly, why did he keep an ordinary silver ring alongside?'

The silver ring was lying in front of him. He was intrigued every time he looked at it. Playing with the ring, there were many thoughts crossing his mind. He felt that surely there must be some secret hidden in this ring. Suddenly, his fingers happened to press on a tiny button on the ring and the ring opened up. He saw that inside the ring there was a tiny piece of paper. He pulled it out, unfolded it and saw four words written on it. When he read the words, he felt that his father had written the essence of his entire life on that small piece of paper.

On that paper his father had written a message. The message was: **'This too shall pass.'**

Deepak contemplated hard over this message and soon he started realizing its meaning – whenever an incident occurs in life, it does not remain the same forever; it changes. Situations that have arisen in life are bound to change, 'this too shall pass.'

On applying this message in his life, Deepak never got entangled in any incident, good or bad. His self-talk never erred. As soon as any negative self-talk would begin inside, he would say to himself, "This too shall pass."

Saying so, the negative self-talk would instinctively stop and he would get on with his work at hand. With this, his present state started getting better, and likewise his future too brightened up. His wealth started increasing, his business flourished.

But his elder brother Sumesh did not have this mantra. His wealth was diminishing and his business was deteriorating day by day. One day in despair Sumesh went to meet his younger brother and grumbled, "Dad has definitely given you something which you have kept to yourself. You have not shared it with me. Your wealth and business are prospering due to it."

"Brother, forgive me" said Deepak laughingly, "What you say is true. Dad gave me an invaluable mantra, due to which my business is thriving."

Now the self-talk within Sumesh started racing – 'Has dad given him a magic wand! What is it that he gave him due to which his business is thriving? Is he telling the truth? Is he trying to fool me? Or is he hiding something from me?'

Deepak then placed the piece of paper in front of Sumesh. Sumesh picked it up with quivering hands. As he read the words 'This too shall pass', the self-talk that occurred in him was, 'He is trying to fool me and cheat me. He is showing me some worthless piece of paper. Dad would have given him something more important and he is hiding that.'

He threw away the paper and screamed, "You are lying to me; dad must have given you something else."

Deepak calmly joined his hands and reverently said, "Brother, this is the mantra that dad gave me."

However, Sumesh was in no mood to listen. He was seething with negative self-talk. With an angry red face, he went away cursing.

This is what happens with us too. We come across so many thoughtful, soul-searching, life-transforming messages but before we understand, we dismiss them due to negative self-talk. From today onwards, we have to remember this message-in-a-ring, this small mantra. Whenever any event occurs in life, be it good or bad, tell yourself, "**This too shall pass.**" This message will prove to be a magical self-talk. As soon as this self-talk begins, negative self-talk will come to an end. In all ups and downs of life, this message will serve you.

10

Fix An Appropriate Price Tag To Every Incident

A young man Rajesh (name changed) came to seek guidance from Sirshree.

Sirshree: So, Rajesh, what brings you here?

As soon as he was asked this question, Rajesh's face cringed with agony.

Rajesh: Sirshree, what do I say? I cannot figure out whether my problem is major or minor, but I am besieged by innumerable thoughts. A peculiar event has taken place and it refuses to go out of my mind. What should I do?

Sirshree: First of all, express your problem in words. For, if a problem is conveyed properly in words, there is a possibility of it getting cleared just by expressing it. You will also feel relieved.

Rajesh: It happened two months ago. I was attending a party hosted by my company. All my colleagues were present. It was evening time. The party was going on in full swing. Everybody was having fun and there was laughter everywhere. People were celebrating in high spirits. I was having food and walking around with my plate when I suddenly slipped. I wasn't hurt but the plate landed on my clothes and I fell onto a heap of used plates. My expensive suit also got soiled.

There was pain and frustration on Rajesh's face as he spoke. His eyes were showing signs of bitterness. Rajesh: I tried to get up carefully but my foot slipped again and I fell for a second time, onto the adjoining lawn. A group of ladies standing nearby burst into laughter. Others too joined in the fun. A waiter meanwhile came and helped me up. When I got to my feet, all the men as well as ladies started poking fun at me. Somebody passed a comment aloud, 'If you cannot take care of yourself, why did you drink so much?' Someone else snidely remarked, 'If you are getting it for free, it doesn't mean you should get drunk to the hilt!' People were taunting me and laughing themselves hoarse.

While saying this, tears were flowing from his eyes. His words had also gathered anger.

Rajesh: Sirshree, I do not take alcohol. I had not taken drinks on that day either. The floor was so slippery in that hall that anybody could have slipped on it. Everyone made fun of me that day. Even later, for days together, they kept on sneering at me saying, 'If you get drinks for free, do you have to drink so much?' I tried telling them that I do not consume alcohol. But nobody was ready to listen. Sirshree, even now I am not able to erase that episode from my mind. It keeps replaying in my mind time and again. I keep thinking on how everybody degraded me. Please tell me, what should I do in this condition?

Rajesh was imploring with hands joined together. There was a brief moment of silence so that Rajesh could compose himself.

Sirshree: Rajesh, just imagine that you have gone to a shop to buy a matchbox. That shopkeeper is selling a matchbox for five rupees. And the neighbouring shopkeeper is selling the same matchbox for one rupee. Will you buy the one costing five rupees?

Rajesh: No, I won't buy it.

Sirshree: Why won't you buy it?

Rajesh: Because it is overpriced. The neighbouring shop is selling it for the right price, and I am in no hurry.

The expression on Rajesh's face revealed that he thought it was such an ordinary matter.

Sirshree: Fine, if that shopkeeper tells you that he is willing to sell it for 2 rupees, will you take it?

Rajesh: (Impatiently) No, why should I? Why should I pay him more than its actual value? I will pay exactly what its value is.

Sirshree: (laughs)

Rajesh: (with surprise) Sirshree, I didn't understand.

Sirshree: Rajesh, you are not willing to pay more than what the actual value for a small matchbox. You want to pay exactly what it is worth. Likewise, in life there are so many incidents that have happened and are happening. What value ought to be given to them, but what value are you giving?

On hearing this, Rajesh's eyes widened. His jaw dropped and with a gaping mouth he looked at Sirshree.

Sirshree: If anybody taunts at you or any other such incident takes place, decide for yourself how much value you are going to give to that incident. By 'value' Sirshree means, how much time are you going to lament over that incident? For how many days are you going to think about it? First decide the worth of that incident. One day, two days, one week, one year, fifty years? How many days' worth of value are you going to give to that event? When you decide its value, give it only that much. Just as you were not ready to pay more money for the matchbox than its actual value, in the same way, do not give the event more value than what it is actually worth. If you decide that the worth of the episode is two days of sorrow, allow yourself to remain sad for two days. Do cry over it for two days. But after two days, do not spend even a single moment crying over it. If your sorrow ends in one and a half days, it is well and good but do not exceed the maximum limit of two days. Whatever self-talk is going on within you about the office girls, about your colleagues and about that particular occurrence, how much longer should it continue? How long will you let the negative self-talk carry on? How long will you remain sulking?"

Rajesh thought for a few moments. Subsequently his eyes shone with a spark of insight.

Rajesh: Now I will not spend even a single moment thinking about that instance because I have already paid a high price for it. (In a decisive tone) Sirshree, that occurrence was worth crying over only for one day. And I, like a fool, spent so many days brooding over it. I consider myself to be business-minded and a practical person and yet I was making such a bad deal.

Thereafter, Rajesh always contemplated over how much value every incident was worth, and paid only as much. He became practical and sensible in his dealings.

We too face various situations in our life. We may be making some mistakes too. Who doesn't? Even the smartest people make mistakes. When mistakes happen, negative self-talk begins within us. We then start cursing either ourselves or others. This disturbs our mental balance. The mind is agitated with resentment and remorse. Hence if there is any past event that is always troubling you, ask yourself, **"How much is this incident worth?"**

We must pay nothing more than what the matchbox (incident) is worth. Remember the word **'matchbox value'**. In every incident, ask yourself, "What is its matchbox value? How many days should

I spend in misery? For how many days must I cry over negative events?"

Likewise, if happy events occur in your life, such as getting an award or receiving praise, you feel jubilant. It is a good thing, however, we tend to get carried away with our emotions and this illusory joy impedes our progress. During those times too, tell yourself,

"This event was quite a pleasant one but for how long should I bask in its glory? One day, two days, one week or one year?" As it is, illusory happiness disappears on its own after some time. You may definitely celebrate for the rightful duration, but after that you need to get back to work. The ecstatic self-talk must be halted right there.

Many a time people achieve some minor success and keep blowing their trumpets over it all their life and continue to inflate their ego. It is good to be happy at your success and share your happiness with others. You deserve to be happy when you have done some good work but if you have to get on with your work, you need to stop your egoistic self-talk. To stop that self-talk, decide its matchbox value. Give only that much what it deserves, not a moment beyond that. By doing so, you will come closer to the present situation and you will start working anew for tomorrow. By deciding the matchbox value, you will pull away from the past and future and be centered in the present. You will begin to go closer to your aim. Otherwise people usually keep oscillating in the self-talk about the past or the future. To snap out of such situations you must definitely use the principle of '**matchbox value**' and firmly hold on to your remote control.

*The boundless energy of my subconcious mind is
aptly guiding me every moment and in every aspect.*

When you take up responsibility
for your sorrows,
you stop complaining about others.
When you can allow yourself
to become sad,
you can also allow yourself
to become happy.
Thus a new understanding
will be born.

SECTION III
HOW TO APPLY THE MAGIC OF SELF-TALK IN VARIOUS FIELDS OF LIFE

When your thoughts gain direction
through self-talk,
you will experience that
you haven't lost your happiness;
it is always with you.

11
Self-talk And Complete Health

Our self-talk has a far-reaching impact on our body and mind. Not everybody knows this and therefore most people unknowingly linger on with negative self-talk. Such self-talk that is repeated very often gets converted into beliefs. It is these beliefs that yield negative results. If someone frequently repeats to himself every day, "I am healthy… I am health", his subconscious mind will start believing in it. When the subconscious mind starts believing something, its results begin to show in our life. With the knowledge of this quality of the subconscious mind, you can achieve whatever you want in life – love, wealth, happiness, satisfaction…

The subconscious mind works according to its old pattern of thinking. It will go about its work in the same manner until we give it a new pattern, a new framework of thinking. Create your new pattern today! Let it be full of love, good health, ample time and immense happiness. Hammer in this new, positive pattern every day (by repeating at least a hundred times) until your subconscious mind is convinced about it. The secret to have your subconscious mind believe in something is 'repetition'. This repetition destroys old patterns and programming. Use this principle to maximum effect and become a new, 'bright' and fresh being. Use positive words and repeat them with ease, confidence and love. Memorize a few lines by heart so that they go straight into the subconscious mind without alerting the conscious mind.

Perform this exercise keeping your body in a relaxed posture. Sit on a comfortable chair or lie down, and give instructions to your mind in an easy, rhythmic manner. The effect of self-talk multiplies tenfold when the body is relaxed. If possible, give a poetic form or rhythm to your new pattern-building self-talk. Recite this poem whenever you have time. Music and rhythm are unmistakable means of reaching into the subconscious mind.

When the body is down with illness, the mind indulges in negative self-talk. It gets upset over trivial matters and becomes distressed in no time. This negative self-talk hinders the body's progress towards recuperation. The body has the inbuilt capacity to heal itself, provided there are no impediments in its way. Negative self-talk is a major impediment on the way to healthy life.

Like the body, the mind too can be afflicted by diseases such as anger, ego, fear, worry, hatred, jealousy and greed. A person afflicted by these diseases of the mind cannot properly digest the food that he consumes. Any such mental defilement which we want to conceal from others, can cause a lot of harm to us. Ego can lead to ailments in the knees. Deceit causes ailments of the throat and lungs. The habit of being stubborn and obstinate can result in ailments of the stomach. By holding onto our stubbornness, we do not even allow for expulsion of the waste inside us. The moment we accept ourselves as we are and feel secure, many of our illnesses are wiped out. Therefore, we must recite the following self-talk to ourselves: *"I accept myself as I am."*

We may be harbouring thoughts which we fear might dent our self-image if revealed to others. By hiding these thoughts inside us, the organs in our body become weak and prone to illnesses. These thoughts play a vital role in promoting diseases. Excessive anger and irritability are injurious for the liver and gallbladder. Fear adversely affects the kidneys and urinary bladder. Stress and worries have harmful effects on the pancreas. Impatience and impulsive behaviour are detrimental to the heart and small intestine. Suppressing sorrow reduces the efficiency of the lungs and large intestine.

It is observed that people afflicted by negative self-talk do not have the will to give anything to others. This miserly attitude hampers the process of expulsion of waste from the intestines (constipation), impairs the proper expulsion of sweat from the skin and prevents complete exhalation of breath from the lungs.

By avoiding negative thoughts and inculcating happy thoughts, we can take good care of our health. The cause of our mental stress must be determined and accepted on time. Taking timely action in the present is in *our* hands. We should not expect others to help us out with this. We should not feel belittled even if someone insults us. Due to insults and traumas suffered during childhood, man lives a closed and constricted life wherein he tends to withdraw in every situation. Owing to this, his body and mind does not develop completely. He is afraid of taking up responsibilities. It is possible that he develops ailments in his legs and shoulders, because legs take us forward and shoulders carry responsibilities. If you happen to have gone through traumas in your childhood, recite the following self-talk:

"I am now ready to move ahead because I have complete faith in the divine plan. I am now ready to shoulder new responsibilities, for which nature is providing me enough courage. I am secure. I am prospering."

Negative self-talk invites diseases and the symptoms appear on the body, which the body then has to suffer. Therefore, stop such negative self-talk. To avoid such diseases, apply and experience the power of positive self-talk. Let this book provide the right direction to your self-talk. Achieve complete health through positive self-talk and self-suggestions.

Curing of diseases will go on, but developing the habit of positive self-talk is very essential. Repeating a particular self-dialogue either in your mind or loudly is called self-reporting.

To bolster the strength of the mind in addition to curing diseases, recite the following self-talk with faith and affection:

"I have learnt the magic of self-talk... I am now recovering. I am in the process of becoming perfect. I am recovering from all my illnesses in quick time. All good and appropriate things are happening in my life according to the divine plan."

Along with this, you can also recite the following: *"Every minute, in every way, my mind and body are getting better and better"* and *"I am God's property, no disease can harm (**touch**) me."*

Whilst utilizing the power of positive self-talk, also try to understand the causes for your ailments. Try to figure out whether the illness has been caused by any inappropriate habit of yours. Check your eating habits, sleeping habits, lack of exercise, etc. If you do not have any vices that could have caused the illness, sit back quietly and check the self-talk that goes on inside you. When there is no physical cause of your illness, the culprit is always your self-talk. To terminate the negative self-talk that obstructs your recovery, recite the following:

"I am now ready to move ahead because I have complete faith in the divine plan. I am now ready to shoulder new responsibilities, for which nature is providing me enough courage. I am secure. I am prospering."

Negative self-talk invites diseases and the symptoms appear on the body, which the body then has to suffer. Therefore, stop such negative self-talk. To avoid such diseases, apply and experience the power of positive self-talk. Let this book provide the right direction to your self-talk. Achieve complete health through positive self-talk and self-suggestions.

Curing of diseases will go on, but developing the habit of positive self-talk is very essential. Repeating a particular self-dialogue either in your mind or loudly is called self-reporting.

To bolster the strength of the mind in addition to curing diseases, recite the following self-talk with faith and affection: *"I have learnt the magic of self-talk... I am now recovering. I am in the process of becoming perfect. I am recovering from all my illnesses in quick time. All good and appropriate things are happening in my life according to the divine plan."*

Along with this, you can also recite the following: *"Every minute, in every way, my mind and body are getting better and better"* and *"I am God's property, no disease can harm (**touch**) me."*

Whilst utilizing the power of positive self-talk, also try to understand the causes for your ailments. Try to figure out whether the illness has been caused by any inappropriate habit of yours. Check your eating habits, sleeping habits, lack of exercise, etc. If you do not have any vices that could have caused the illness, sit back quietly and check the self-talk that goes on inside you. When there is no physical cause of your illness, the culprit is always your self-talk. To terminate the negative self-talk that obstructs your recovery, recite the following:

"I am now ready to give up the thought pattern of my contrast mind (misapprehension, wrong conviction or false belief) which has created this situation (illness). I am now free; I am freedom... I am happy, I am happiness..."

Hammer in this new thinking pattern (happy thoughts) repeatedly every day. In the end, herald the end of your illness by declaring once more: *"I am free... I am freedom... I am happy... I am happiness..."* Repeat this self-dialogue daily, whenever you get a chance.

Visualize that you are going through the process of recuperation and you are experiencing the feeling of wellbeing within you. Whenever required, recite the following words/happy thoughts/self-suggestions:

"I am free from negative self-talk. I have become calm and peaceful. I believe in life, I am secure. I am experiencing the happiness created by my new, positive thinking pattern. I am calm... I am important... I am complete... I love and accept myself. I am worthy of being loved. I am feeling fresh. I care for my body and mind with affection. I am accepting and expressing the happiness of life. I believe that everything happening in my life is always apt. I am Consciousness... I am flowing happily with every experience of life. Everything is going on just fine. I gladly set free my past and now I am relaxed. I now live in the present. My life is overflowing with happiness. Joyous thoughts are brimming inside me."

Record the above self-talk in your own voice. Play this audio record to yourself once a day when you are in a relaxed state of mind and body, preferably in *shavasana*. *Shavasana* is a posture in yoga. It is the most important and effective posture in yoga to relax your body. It soothes and releases strain from the body and stress from the mind. Lay a carpet or a sheet on the floor and lie down on it. Let your body loose, as if a corpse is laid on the floor. The complete procedure is described below:

1. Lie down on your back.
2. Keep a distance of 12 to 18 inches between your feet. Also place your hands 8 to 12 inches away from your torso. Relax your body.

3. Keep your head still. Tilt it slightly towards your right or left, or else face straight towards the ceiling as per your convenience. Close your eyes.

4. Using your willpower and imagination, relax your body. It is very important to relax each and every part of your body.

5. Let your breathing be normal. Concentrate your mind on your heart without applying too much effort.

6. Stay in this state for 15 to 20 minutes. Do not allow drowsiness to creep in. Learn the art of relaxing your body.

Shavasana has many benefits. Due to relaxation of the body and mind, blood circulation is improved. *Shavasana* is particularly beneficial for heart patients. Those suffering from heart ailments, hypertension and physical or mental stress should make it a point to practice *shavasana*.

Apart from *shavasana*, there is another method which you can follow. Select one or two powerful self-suggestions. Write them down around 10 to 20 times every day and recite them aloud. Give a rhythm to these suggestions and hum them happily. Let your brain dwell on these thoughts the entire day. Strong thoughts when repeated constantly turn into reality. Sometimes the results you get can be phenomenal and simply beyond your imagination.

You have learnt the method of keeping your body and mind healthy. You can use the same technique to attain spiritual wellbeing. With the power of persistent positive self-talk and self-suggestions, you can courageously walk the path of Truth, destroying all your patterns, tendencies, negative programming and habits on the way. When you are able to do this, you will achieve 'complete health'.

12

How To Regain Your Remote Control

If you were to be asked whether there should be an aim in life, the answer would be in the affirmative, "Yes! There ought to be an aim in life." Now the question that arises is, "Do I really have an aim in my life? Have I ever thought as to what should happen at the end of my life which would make me feel that my life has indeed been successful?" This question is worth contemplating upon.

Let us leave aside the question of what should happen at the end of your life for the time being. Have you at least thought about what you should be doing in the next six months or in the next one year, so as to feel that your life has been successful? If your life has no aim how will it be successful? Everyone has his life, but there are very few who attain the true aim in life.

Suppose that you are told, "Get a good cricket bowler from anywhere in the world. We will do something that will soon make him forget his bowling. He will quit bowling and go away. Bring in some good cricket fielders and you go in for batting. However, the bowler will not be able to get you 'out'; instead, he himself will get 'out'!" You will ask, "How? How is this possible?"

Yes! It is possible. We will give him the ball and bring him on, but we will remove the three stumps at which he normally bowls. Without stumps in front of him, what will the bowler bowl at? How long will he continue to bowl? He will give up bowling and leave within a short time.

Similarly, it is essential that we too have 'stumps' in our life. If a good cricket bowler is not able to see the stumps, how will he be able to bowl? Likewise, do we have 'stumps' to look at in our life? In other words, **do we have an aim in life?** If we do not have any aim in life, all the vigour and potential within us is wasted. Despite having strength, no bowler can bowl without stumps in front of him. He needs to be able to see the stumps in order to bowl. In the same way, we may have immense strength and talent within us, but it is also important to have an aim (direction). This is not for us alone; do our family members have 'stumps' in their life? Do our children have them? Do our colleagues and assistants at work have them? And are they able to see their aim at all times?

Many a time, you may feel that you have achieved your aim; but yet you feel a void, an emptiness within. This is because you do not know that there is always a larger aim behind every aim.

You may have experienced very often that despite achieving everything you wanted, you still feel that 'there is something missing in my life, something that is unfulfilled as yet'. Why do you feel so? The reason is that behind the aim that you pursue, there is another purpose which you do not perceive. What is the aim that you should have, and what is the aim beyond this aim can be understood by a little story that follows.

> There was a man who had an infant son. He used to always think about his son. He used to feel that his son should progress rapidly. Every parent feels the same way. But this

father had very tall hopes. He felt that his son should be able to climb up a hill and reach the temple at its summit. But the child, being a little infant, could not even walk a few steps straight. He was only just learning to crawl.

The father then thought of an idea to help his child develop the ability to walk and to climb up and down the hill. He chalked out a plan for him. He dug up two pits at some distance from each other and drew a line in between them. He tossed up a nice colourful ball to his kid and told him, "Take this ball, throw it once in this direction from behind the line into one pit... then throw it in the other direction into the other pit from the other side of the line."

He explained all the rules to him. Now the kid started playing. Happily, he threw the ball alternately into each of the pits. While playing, he was actually learning to walk. We all know what happens when toddlers learn to walk. Do they walk or fall more often? You would say, "They fall more often." A question then arises, "So what are they learning – walking or falling?" You would reply, "They are obviously learning how to walk." Trivial failures like falling do not dissuade them from their aim.

But it is not the same with us. When failures befall upon us, we think of quitting in disappointment. Children do not quit. A lot happens during our day at work, but what are the instances that our mind clings onto? We do not latch onto the happy moments that we experience. We hold on to insults, derogation and other such negative things that we have had to endure sometime during the day. What are the thoughts that run through your mind when you are treated badly? Stop and ponder for a while.

Some of the thoughts that pass through your mind would be, 'How can he say such a thing to me? What does he think of himself? I will settle the score with him tomorrow... I will make him look like a fool...'

This is brought out in the following anecdote. One day, a neighbour ridiculed Raju in front of several people by calling him a hippo. Everybody had a laugh and Raju too went away with a grin on his face. Actually, he did not know what a hippo was. It is only when Raju visited the zoo after a couple of days and saw a hippopotamus that he started fuming with rage. It was then that he understood why everybody was laughing at him on being called a hippo. His self-talk started after two days, only when he saw the animal. Though he had heard the word two days ago, anger started brewing within him only when he saw the hippopotamus. The self-talk that ensued flared up his fury. He said to himself, "How dare he call me a hippo! Let him come before me... I'll call him a dinosaur! I will call him a wild dinosaur, aloud, and that too in front of many people."

This is exactly what happens with us. We tend to hold on to negative happenings and the turmoil lasts for several days. In addition to negative incidents, we also tend to linger in past appreciation.

Suppose somebody praises you and says, "You made this possible. Without you, it wouldn't have been possible." Now when you are appreciated so much, check the effect it has on you. In such situations, there are many who would not be able to sleep. They will keep ruminating over the appreciation they received all through the night. The self-talk goes on endlessly.

Can you decipher what this means? We need to contemplate upon what this implies. It means that our *remote-control* is in others' hands. Imagine that we, our feelings, can be controlled by a remote-control. In many situations, we hand over our remote-control to others. They press the buttons on the remote-control and we helplessly react accordingly. If somebody points out faults in our work, we start feeling agitated. If somebody praises us, we feel happy. Thus we hand over our remote-control to others and then keep hoping that they would press the button of appreciation, and not that of criticism or anger.

But then, what should ideally happen? **Your remote-control should firmly be in your own hands, every moment.** You should not let external circumstances, external events or others' talk disturb you and ruffle your composure. The prime aim of this book is to teach you how to hold on to your remote-control at all times through the technique of self-talk.

Little children are not affected by external happenings. Minor failures do not dampen their spirits. To continue with the tale of the toddler learning how to walk, he was throwing the ball into the pit, retrieving it and throwing it again. By doing so, he was actually learning how to walk and run. By throwing the ball into the pits repeatedly, he gained expertise in it. Ninety out of hundred times, he could throw the ball into the pit. When the ball fell into the pit he would cheer up in glee and exclaim, "I won, I won…!" When the ball did not go into the pit, he would say, "Oh no! I've lost."

Now this child had become entrapped in the process. He now believed that it was vitally important that the ball went into the pit. According to his father's plan, it was not at all important how many times the ball went into the pit. Whether it went in ten times or a hundred times, it did not really matter. What mattered was that in and through this *play*, the kid was learning how to walk and run. The skill of walking was to be utilized towards a larger aim – that of climbing up the hill!

The same thing happens in our life. We give more importance to winning and losing during difficulties. Due to this, we lose sight of the bigger aim (the aim beyond aim). Difficulties will arise; but winning and losing during these difficulties is not very important. What is important is that during these difficulties we must firmly hold on to our remote-control.

Coming out of the problem is the aim. **The aim beyond this aim is to develop some skills and make our mind unswerving and pure.**

It is important to know where our remote-control lies every moment. If we are unsuccessful at something, what is our self-talk like? Ensure that your remote-control is in your own hands at all times. If you are able to acquire this art, you will win in the truest sense of the word. Otherwise you lose; despite appearing to others as if you have won. If you do not improve on your efficiency, capability, skill, talent and understanding, it can be inferred that you have actually lost, although you may appear to have won.

If you have been able to comprehend this entire subject, you will henceforth win twice in every problem – once by overcoming the problem, and more importantly by achieving the aim beyond aim.

I am in harmoney with life.
I am receiving something new every day, every moment.

13

How You Can Change The Entire World

Once a king of an empire was suffering from a strange kind of illness. Nobody had a cure for this illness. After a long search, the king finally found a physician who claimed that he could cure his disease. The remedy that he prescribed to the king seemed weird, but everyone decided to go by it – after all, it was their only hope.

The physician said, "The more the king sees red colour around him, the faster will he recover from his ailment." Upon hearing this, the king ordered for all the places that he visited or passed by to be set up in such a way that he would see only red colour, whatever he set his eyes upon.

People immediately got down to work. All the walls were painted red… the roads by which the king used to pass were decked with red curtains and carpets. The soldiers and guards changed into a red uniform. The king's throne and the entire courtroom were turned into red.

The process of painting the town red was in full swing, so much so that skilled labour from outside the kingdom had to be hired to cope with this workload. As every object in the kingdom was turning into red, the royal treasury was fast depleting. In and through this process, people were happy to see the king recovering from his illness. Looking at the positive results, all the houses around the palace were ordered to be painted red. Red was reigning, but the royal treasury was draining!

Looking at all the flurry, a small boy in the neighbourhood was baffled. He went straight to the courtroom and asked the king, "What are you doing! Why are you spending so much money?" People were taken aback and feared for the child. The chief of the ministers rose to his feet and shouted at the child, "How dare you? Who are you to ask this question? The king's health is more important than the wealth. You probably do not wish for the speedy recovery of the king. Looking at your teeny age we are letting you go, otherwise any other person would have been arrested for this misconduct."

The child calmly replied, "I too wish that the king should recover quickly, but I do not approve of these methods. If you give me a chance to speak, I have a solution that is not as expensive."

"Get out of here!" the minister retorted angrily. "What solution can you have that wise pundits and physicians cannot think of? Go away or else you will be jailed." The child started to leave when the king stopped him and said, "Everyone in this courtroom is equal and should be given a fair chance. Though the probability of you having a solution is very less, I shall still give you one chance. Say what you have to say."

"Thank you, Your Highness!" the child responded politely. "I had only heard of you before, but today I have got the opportunity to see you. It is probably due to this way of dealing with matters that people respect you so! No wonder everybody is working hard for your recovery. But I have a solution that will cure your illness at a negligible cost." Having said this, the child handed over a pair of spectacles with red-coloured glasses to the king. With the red glasses on, the king could see everything as red. The whole courtroom stood up and applauded.

"I bought them in a fair," said the child. "With these on, everything you see will appear to be red in colour. You will recover in quick time and also save a lot of money." People were amazed at the child's wit.

We also look through coloured glasses. It is but natural that whatever colour glasses we wear, the world appears to be of the same colour to us. Likewise, the kind of self-talk that goes on within us determines the way we feel about the world. Self-talk is like a pair of spectacles for the mind. If we look at a person through yellow glasses, he will appear to be yellow. If seen through black glasses, he will appear to be black.

On many occasions, we set out to change the world, much like the king in the story. We set out to change other people. We focus on *their* mistakes. **But if we change our own spectacles (our self-talk), *our* entire world will change at once.** Now it is up to us to decide the colour of glasses that we want to wear on our mind. In other words, we need to choose what kind of self-talk we should adopt in any situation.

The best thing to do is to not put on any glasses at all (be open-minded and in silence). If at all glasses *have* to be put on, use colourless, transparent glasses so that we see everything as it actually is, without any prejudices.

In life, we come across various types of people. Each person evokes different feelings in our mind. It is depending on these feelings that we decide how to interact with that person. Our approach towards interacting with any person is influenced by two aspects; firstly, the number of times we have met the person earlier, and secondly, the incidents that have occurred whenever we have met him. If the incidents that have occurred during previous encounters have been positive, we tend to adopt a positive attitude towards him. We put together these incidents and draw up an image of that person in our mind. The self-talk that is triggered upon seeing that person determines our reaction towards him.

It is a common fact that no two people interact in exactly the same manner with any person. Looking at ourselves, we can notice that we too do not interact with everybody in the same manner. Neither does everyone else behave in the same manner with us. Man interacts differently with different people. Someone might behave very well with you, but the very next moment he could scowl at somebody else. We may have also observed that some people speak ill of the same person whom *we* regard as being very nice.

At the workplace, there are some people who despise the mere sight of their boss. Some people even hope that their boss does not show up at the office for the day. But if you have a look at the situation at the boss's house, you might see a totally different picture. Perhaps someone would be waiting for him. Probably his son would be longing to spend some time with his father and therefore would be asking him to take a day's leave from the office.

How is it that opinions about the same person vary to such an extent? How is it that people draw such variety of images about him? There are people who think well about a person and there are also others who think ill about him. This proves that **whenever we encounter a person our self-talk is triggered; and it is this self-talk that decides *for us* whether the person is good or bad.**

Every person appears different to different people because he plays different roles in each of their lives. Somebody may be a boss at the workplace, but at home he may be a husband, a father, a brother or a son. As he shifts through his roles, his behaviour changes accordingly. Based on his behaviour, people form opinions about him. Someone may think that he is lovable while someone else may deem that he is quite strict, somebody might believe that he is helpful, whereas somebody else may feel that he is humorous. The person is the same, yet the way we perceive him is more important. Let us understand this with the help of the following story.

Once upon a time, there was a sudden heavy downpour in a village. Some people took shelter under a huge tree. Within a short time, quite a few people of all ages and occupations had assembled below the canopy. There was also a hermit among them. Upon seeing the hermit, everybody started asking him questions about their life. Though all their questions seemed to be different, they all pointed towards the same thing. Their questions were like, "Why do people behave badly…? Why the world is made this way…? Why don't people understand me…? Why are people so selfish…?"

The hermit replied, "You will get all your answers, but before that, all of you have to give an answer to my question. Tell me what thoughts appeared in your mind on seeing this tree under which we all have taken refuge? What do you feel looking at this tree?"

A young student among them answered, "There's a big tree like this illustrated in one of our books. Such trees provide us with oxygen. They also bear fruits that are tasty to eat."

"I am grateful that I found this tree, else I would have fallen sick," said a frail looking man. "This tree has saved me from imminent cough and cold. This tree also protects us from the sun."

"The leaves of this tree have medicinal value and can be used for making life-saving medicines," informed a doctor among them. "This tree is very beneficial for us."

A businessman dealing in wood said, "I can tell from my experience that the wood of this tree is of premium quality. This wood can be

used for making several wooden articles. This is quite an exceptional and rare tree indeed."

Another businessman said, "If we protect this tree from being cut, it will serve us for a lifetime. The fruits of this tree can be sold and the money can help sustain us."

One of them gave a strange answer. He said, "O hermit! What can I hide from you? I am a thief. I was searching for a place in this tree where I can hide while I am on the run."

There was also an artist who said, "This tree is so beautiful! I can envision images taking shape in this tree. One of the branches reminds me of the dome of a temple, while another one reminds me of an elephant's trunk. From one angle I can visualize a little child, while from another I can visualize an old man."

Upon hearing all these answers, the hermit broke out into laughter and explained, "If you get so many different ideas by merely looking at something as gross as a tree, it is but natural that the same will happen when you consider people around you. It is obvious that different people will evoke different thoughts in our mind. Therefore, **before forming an opinion about any person, ask yourself whether that person is really like what you think of him to be and whether others too think likewise about him... or is it only your imagination?** This question will at once dispel all the pain, discomfort and anxiety caused by the irrational behaviour of people. You will then adopt a fresh outlook when you meet any person and thus improve your relationships, instead of continuing with preconceived notions about that person. If you change your outlook, thoughts and *dark* spectacles, i.e. if you change your self-talk, the whole world will change for you at once, right now."

14

Self-talk And Body Language

Your victory does not merely depend on what you think of yourself, nor does it depend only on what you have achieved in life so far. Your success depends on what your colleagues at work and people at home think about your character, your nature, commitment and conduct.

If we learn the right use of self-talk, our relations with our family and other people in our life will improve significantly. First we must understand how our relations can improve. To begin with, it is important to know what type of dialogue we wish to have with our colleagues and other people around us.

During a self-development course, a group was asked, "If ten people are working with you, tell me how many hands are working for you?"

"Twenty" was the unanimous answer.

"How?"

"There are ten people, each having two hands, so twenty hands are working for us," said everyone.

"Why just twenty? Why not twenty-two? Look, there are ten people with you, so they count up to twenty hands. But where are your pair of hands? Shouldn't they be included too? That makes it twenty-two hands."

We forget ourselves in such situations. We converse with everyone else, but we forget the conversation with ourselves (our self-talk). It is this self-talk that yields positive or negative results while working in teams or dealing with a group. This self-talk ought to change.

If your self-talk regarding people around you is positive, you will feel more energetic and lively in their presence. However, if your self-talk is negative, your enthusiasm will be sapped out and your energy levels will diminish.

Neelaram and Leelaram were two magicians. Both of them performed the same tricks. Their shows were almost identical. Both of them had the same level of knowledge and skill. But there was one difference. Before starting the show, Neelaram would think to himself, 'How many people will turn up today…? Will the theatre be packed to capacity or not…? How much will I earn today…?' When he would begin with his show, he would think, 'Do these people have any idea about how great a magician I am! I will now show them a trick that will knock the wits out of them. Nobody will be able to spot my sleight-of-hand. Now look how I make fools out of them.'

This kind of self-talk would go on in Neelaram's mind during the whole show. When nobody could spot his trick, he would immediately think to himself, 'Look at these fools!'

The other magician, Leelaram, would perform the same set of tricks, but he was far more popular than Neelaram. During the show, the self-talk in Leelaram's mind would be, "These people must have had a tiring day at work or at home. Some of them may even be stressed. My job is to provide them with three hours of fun and entertainment. They should forget their worries and go home happy and refreshed."

Leelaram would also think, 'When people see my show they should get motivated. They should be stirred into thinking on the secrets of life. They should get back to the laughing and playing ways in their life.'

What is depicted by the self-talk of these magicians? Whose show will people prefer to see? The one who's self-talk is negative? Or the one who's self-talk is positive?

The person who's self-talk about the people around him is positive and optimistic, creates positive vibrations. These vibrations reach across to the people in contact with him. **We create the same kind of vibrations around us as the kind of self-talk that we persist with. And these vibrations either attract people or repel them.**

Leelaram's magic shows gained popularity by the day while Neelaram was losing his recognition. Neelaram was clueless as to why this was happening. He was left wondering, 'Leelaram performs the same tricks that I do; everything is the same. On the contrary, my stage decorations are better. Then why is it that Leelaram attracts such crowds?' His self-talk now became all the more negative and he soon faded into oblivion.

Now, think for yourself. How is your self-talk about the people whom you stay with or about people at your workplace? And how should it ideally be? Follow this practice from today onwards. Every morning, when you wake up, repeat the following self-talk: *"Today, my family is going to be happy because of me and so will my colleagues at work who will be delighted with me. My positive self-talk and conversation is going to make them enjoy their work."*

What exactly happens when we alter our self-talk? Our self-talk reveals itself in the form of our body language. Our body language is like an unspoken communication that gets instantly conveyed to the subconscious mind of people around us. Negative body language instantly creates strain, withdrawal and aversion in them. Positive body language impresses the subconscious mind of one and all. Everyone begins to co-operate with us. As our self-talk changes, our actions too change accordingly. This happens at a very subtle plane due to which we cannot perceive that it is happening. Therefore, control your self-talk so as to change your body language.

A few years ago, on a Sunday evening, a young man Anmol (name changed) came to participate in Satsang and to seek guidance.

"Sirshree, tomorrow I am going to submit my resignation in my office."

He pulled out an envelope from his pocket and said, "Sirshree, this is my resignation letter. Tomorrow I am going to place it on my boss's desk."

Sirshree asked him whether he had got a new job.

On being asked this question, Anmol's face filled with anger. A look of vengeance could be seen on his face.

"No, Sirshree, I haven't got a new job. But you don't know about the trouble my boss has given me during the last one year! I am fed up of him. Tomorrow, I will place this resignation letter before him, get his signature of approval, and go to Accounts department to settle my outstanding dues and clearance. Then, I will go back to meet my boss..."

By now, Anmol's eyes were spitting venom. He continued, "I will meet my boss, not for shaking hands with him... instead I will give him a tight slap across his face."

As soon as he said these words, a wicked smile appeared on his face. He seemed to experience a sadistic pleasure. Anmol concluded, "When I slap him hard, I will feel a sense of satisfaction. I am resigning in order to avenge all the hardships he has put me through all these days."

Sirshree said, "That's fine Anmol. No problem with that. Do what you feel like. But before that, do just one thing that Sirshree tells you for the next fifteen days. This will help everyone, and most of all it will help you."

"But I am going to resign", said Anmol.

"You may resign, but after fifteen days. Before that you have to do one small thing."

There was a question mark on Anmol's face. He looked up uncertainly. He was thinking, 'what is it that I will be told?' He wore a look that demonstrated his suspicious tendency.

Sirshree continued, "If you have faith in the Truth that is expounded here, you have to do just one thing for the next fifteen days... you have to pray twice a day, once in the morning and once in the evening."

"If you say so, I'll definitely do that."

"You have to pray, but *for your boss*."

Anmol was taken aback and also a bit angry.

"Why? Why should I pray for him?" asked Anmol in a frustrated tone.

"We shall talk about that after fifteen days. What you have to do now is pray. Pray that your boss gets everything he wants... all his wishes are fulfilled... his health is revitalized... he becomes peaceful physically and mentally with every passing day... and that he progresses financially. Along with this, also pray that he attains happiness every day in his life and that he achieves all his aims."

"What are you telling me to do?! I don't think I'll be able to do that *ever*."

"Anmol, this is just an experiment. Why don't you try it? In any case, you are going to resign."

"Okay Sirshree, I'll do it only because you are telling me to," Anmol agreed reluctantly.

After a fortnight, Anmol was back for a Sunday session.

" How are you, Anmol? When are you tendering your resignation?" Sirshree asked.

This time Anmol had a different expression. In fact, he even had a slight smile on his face.

"Sirshree, I am rethinking on my decision to resign. Strangely, these days, my boss has started behaving very nicely with me. I don't know what has happened! I cannot understand how he can speak so well with me!"

Everybody in the session burst into laughter.

"Haven't you guessed as yet how this has come about? It all depends on the self-talk that goes on within us. You started praying for your boss which had an immediate effect on your self-talk. When your self-talk changes, when your thoughts change, your manner of speaking also begins to change. Not only does your speech change, but your body language also begins to change. Your body language just cannot remain negative towards the person for whom you are praying day and night. Your body language will always be positive for him. Your positive vibrations are picked up by the subconscious mind of that person. Then he too starts giving you a similar response."

This is how it always works. Be it a magician or a boss, a neighbour or your mother-in-law... it is always you who has to change first in order to effect change in them. You will change by altering your self-talk. **If you change your self-talk, you will find that the people with whom you deal begin to change too.** Their approach towards you and their style of speaking with you will be seen to change.

You may be an employee fed up of your boss... you may be married and fed up of your in-laws... you could be a gentleman fed up of your neighbour, or a student fed up of your teacher... or the other way round. You must change your body language that gives out wrong impressions. To change your body language, you must change your self-talk. If every neighbour, every friend, every relative and every president of the world changes his self-talk and everyone prays for each other, all relations including those between nations will be rid of hatred! Isn't this the magic of self-talk?!

> *I let go of my insistence and associated stress*
> *that I should always be right.*
> *I perform the right tasks at the right time with ease.*

15

Get Rid Of Grief Resulting From Outflow Of Money

People often complain that they are not able to save money and that they are always faced with shortage of funds.

Some people even say that if they have a single currency note of denomination five hundred or thousand rupees, it remains intact in their wallet for days together. However, the moment that note is exchanged for smaller units, they get spent in no time!

Some people say that a tacked bundle of currency notes of hundred or five hundred each remains secure with them only until they remain tacked. The moment they are loosened; the money is spent before they realize.

Why does this happen? The reason behind this is our self-talk – wrong self-talk regarding money. People generally tend to complain about their bills and expenses and say, "Look at the electricity bill… it is a thousand rupees this time." Some say, "I filled fuel worth five hundred in the car… and (*sadly*) that's five hundred more gone!" After dining out in a restaurant the husband grumbles, "Look, five hundred wasted! We could have had dinner at home instead." Ladies complain, "I got just two dresses and two thousand rupees are gone!"

Where is everybody's focus? We spend some money every day to buy a few things for us and then groan, "So much money's gone!" But we never think about what we have received in exchange for that money. Whenever we have spent money, we have definitely *received* something for it. When we fill fuel and pay five hundred for it, it is true that we give money; but it is equally true that we receive fuel, which facilitates our comfortable travel from place to place. We tend to neglect this aspect. We pay money to the clothes retailer, but also receive a nice apparel in return. Money may be spent during a family outing, but in return we get good food, joy and satisfaction for the family as well as better bonding with our children. But our focus tends to be on, "What is gone...?" Negative self-talk ceaselessly carries on, "I had this... I had that... now it is all spent..."

Your focus should instead be on, "What have I received?" **In this world, whenever you give something, you receive something in return for sure.** Your money is never wasted; you always get something for it.

You will always spend money; in fact, you earn money to spend it. However, your focus should be on what you receive. This does not imply that you should blow away your money or squander it on frivolous pursuits and extravagances. You have to tread the middle path and learn how to make the best use of your money. If your self-talk regarding money matters is properly directed, it will bring you happiness and show you the way to a good future. However, if your self-talk goes in the wrong direction, i.e. you regret the outflow of money, you will get nothing but grief and the ominous burden of the future. The right self-talk about money will alleviate any such repentance and instead give you joy in the same situation that used to trouble you earlier.

We know that a happy person can never be a cause of sorrow for anyone. The one whose self-talk is heading towards happiness will always remain happy. But if one's self-talk focuses on what he has lost or given away, he is bound to be depressed. On buying a book, is it better to say, "There goes another hundred!" or "Received a good book – an opportunity to gain knowledge"? If you visit a doctor, is it better to say, "More money spent!" or "I will be healthy again"? How should your self-talk be on every occasion? Your self-talk should always focus on positive aspects. This is the secret of financial prosperity.

A gentleman once narrated an incident. "I had been to Mumbai. I was traveling by the suburban train when someone robbed my wallet. The wallet contained a thousand rupees. Given that I have lost a thousand rupees, won't my self-talk be negative?"

What do you feel on reading this? Was he right in saying so? In this instance, money was taken away and nothing was received in return. Is that what you are thinking?

No, you cannot say that "money was taken away and there was nothing received in return." Did you not get a stern lesson on where you ought to keep your money and where not to? Did you not benefit from the experience and learn an important lesson in the process? **We have come to Earth to learn various lessons.** Some lessons are to be learnt the hard way, through knocks and shocks that wake us up. Never get into the wrong habit of giving knocks back to the world upon receiving them. Train your self-talk to offer your gratitude to such jolts that you receive in life because they will only help in your growth.

16

Consider Your Work To Be Your Workout Regimen

We might feel that all of us relate to incidents happening around us in the same manner. But it is not so. Different people see the same incident from different perspectives and experience it differently. After the incident has occurred, the self-talk that takes place in different people is different. Due to this, different people relate differently to an incident although it may appear to be the same externally.

Have you seen a porter lifting heavy luggage? When he is lifting the luggage, what would be the self-talk going on in his mind? He could be thinking, 'Why do I have to pick up others' burden? Why do people travel with so much luggage? My life is so difficult.'

And have you seen a weightlifter picking up weights? He is also lifting heavy objects, but what would his self-talk be? He would most likely be thinking, 'I have to build up my body… Picking up weights will boost my capacity… I will be able to lift heavier weights… I want to be the world's best weightlifter!' When the weightlifter carries such a perspective he becomes stronger by the day.

The same work that is considered by the porter to be a burden is seen as a means to build up muscle by the weightlifter. Though the activity seems to be the same externally, yet it has different effects on these two people. The different effects are caused by the difference in their self-talk while they are engaged in the activity. When the porter sees sweat trickling down his body, he thinks that he is toiling hard like a donkey. When the weightlifter sees his perspiration he thinks, 'Each drop of sweat counts; it is building up my stamina. Tomorrow I will generate more sweat. This is the acknowledgement of my efforts.'

Even the clothes of the porter depict his negative self-talk; whereas the costume of a weightlifter reminds him of his mighty physique. If we observe closely, both of them are doing the same kind of activity. The difference is only in their self-talk related to that activity. This difference attracts illnesses towards the porter and great health towards the weightlifter.

Now observe yourself while you are at work. Ask yourself the question, "With the work that I am engaged in right now, am I relating to it like a porter or like a weightlifter?" This is important because our self-talk has an effect not only on our physical progress, but also in every other aspect of life such as mental, social, spiritual and even financial progress.

Two companies manufacturing footwear once sent their sales representatives to Africa. Both of them were assigned to go to interior Africa and assess their company's prospects of selling footwear in that part of the world.

As soon as these salesmen reached Africa, they were astonished to see that nobody in interior Africa wore any kind of footwear. The salesman of the first company immediately called up his office and informed, "There is no concept of footwear out here. They don't even know what 'shoes' are! Nobody will buy our footwear here. I am taking the next flight home."

The salesman of the other company also called up his office. He reported, "There is no concept of footwear out here. They don't even know what 'shoes' are! This is a wonderful opportunity! I am explaining them the importance of wearing shoes. Everybody here is willing to buy shoes from us. Send a big consignment of shoes as early as possible. Also raise our production volumes to address the demand here. There's a lot of work to be done; I may need to stay longer. Please also send some staff to assist me."

Here, both the salesmen faced the same situation. Their reaction to the situation was not just different, but totally opposite. **Whenever you come across such situations in life, ask yourself whether you want to escape from the scene or stay there and use the situation as an opportunity for growth.** On most occasions, people find very good excuses to avoid situations at work.

We might have heard people saying, "If only I was born in the West… if only I was born in a rich family… if only the market was booming… I would have definitely done something… I am born in the wrong era; if only I was born earlier I too would have made great discoveries. Now there is nothing left to be discovered. Also, we hardly get any freedom at work these days. If only I was born during the times of Newton, Edison or James Watt; I too would have come up with great ideas. There's nothing remaining to be discovered today!"

An interior decorator once complained that although he was very creative and could churn out novel designs, he was still distraught. He grumbled, "How many times must I repeat the same thing again and again? Isn't there a limit?! I have shown a client seven different designs for his home furniture. Whenever I would go with a new design he would say that he wanted something different. Now, how many times should I rework the design? I am fed up… I have quit his project."

People who think like those in the two examples given above should be told, "Either stop comparing yourself with past scientists or start emulating them fully." It is said about Edison that he had to try out 10,000 different experiments before achieving the invention of electricity. When somebody pointed out to him that 9,999 of his experiments had failed, he gave a wonderful answer. He said, "These experiments have not been unsuccessful! I have learnt 9,999 ways by which electricity cannot be generated. Just as 'knowing what to do' implies success, similarly 'knowing what *not* to do' is also a kind of success!"

Probably it is this kind of self-talk that motivated him to carry out so many experiments. If the interior decorator were to take a cue from Edison, he would not have stopped at seven experiments. In this age too, there are so many things yet to be discovered. We too must keep on with new experiments and maintain a positive self-talk while being engaged in our experimentation.

*I am complete; everything gets completed
by me on time.*

17

Learn To Finish Your Tasks Completely

You may have seen several people who have the talent and capability but are unable to utilize their worth to good benefit in their lives. There are many who cannot work efficiently despite having the skill. Among those who have the skill, there are some who have the required competence while there are others who lack it.

The prime reason behind possessing competence or the lack of it is 'self-talk'. It is self-talk that decides the level of capability. The following example illustrates this.

There were two people in a company who were selected for the managerial cadre. One of them was Mr. Macey. He was a chaotic and confused man whose work was always in a state of disarray. The other was Mr. Spick. He always efficiently went about his work in an orderly manner. He was very meticulous at work. He had several achievements under his belt owing to his pragmatic and methodical approach.

Both of them were evaluated for competence and productivity. Before assessing them, their style of working was observed.

Mr. Macey left all his tasks unfinished. He fumbled with almost all his jobs. When he used to start working on a given task, he would be bogged down with the task to such an extent that he would leave all other tasks pending. Although he would perform the given task very well, his other tasks used to remain incomplete.

Mr. Spick always brought all his tasks to completion within committed timelines. He possessed excellent time management skills. Another thing to his credit was that his entire staff was happy with him.

What would happen with Mr. Macey? With every task that he took up, a handful of his staff would be happy while the others would be upset. Again, this situation kept changing with every task as he could not manage to keep any of his staff members satisfied consistently.

Mr. Macey was frustrated with himself as well. He used to grumble to himself, 'I'm always late for the office… And then I bungle up… I forget to get the papers I had removed from my briefcase and reach office without them. I forget to carry my cell phone so often. Sometimes I forget to take the car keys and realize it only when I reach the car… I then need to rush upstairs just to retrieve the keys…'

On waking up in the morning, Mr. Macey would be flooded with thoughts like, 'I need to rush to office early… need to get ready soon… have to gobble up the breakfast… I have not even readied my briefcase…' Thus he would be caught up in his own directionless self-talk. If he had to leave for office by nine o'clock, from eight o'clock onwards he would be immersed in thoughts like, 'Got to leave for office early… Shouldn't forget the briefcase… Which files should I carry with me…? What are my appointments today…?' Thus he would go all around with his nagging self-talk. After reaching his office he would vacillate, 'Today I have got to complete this task… I also need to start with that other task…' This kind of self-talk would ceaselessly go on within him.

With Mr. Spick, it was exactly the opposite. His self-talk would always be properly directed. The self-talk of both of them was analysed. Mr. Macey was asked to train himself by changing his self-talk. He was asked to incorporate Mr. Spick's habits and ways on trial for a week. He was suggested, "Whenever you set out to do anything, contemplate on what things are of priority. If you decide to leave for office at 9 o'clock in the morning, you must have your bath much before that. Before going for your bath, think about what things you will need in the bathroom. Towel, clothes, etc. should be taken along. While bathing or shaving, decide which clothes you will need to wear to office today. Make it a practice not to come out of the bathroom before deciding on this. While you wear your clothes, you may think about the things you need to carry to office. Place them in your briefcase immediately… only then should you have your breakfast. During breakfast, tell yourself that you will take every thought to its completion. Now think about which route you will choose to travel to office. If you have three choices, which one will take you quicker to office? Think about which route is less congested and decide, get up from your breakfast table and leave. Thus, complete each of your tasks fully. When you reach office, give the first ten minutes to yourself. Don't allow anyone to disturb you. In those ten minutes, think about the three most important things you ought to do today."

After training himself in proper self-talk for a week, Mr. Masey found that his valuable time was not getting wasted in unwanted thoughts such as, 'I have to complete this… I also need to do that…' **Incomplete self-talk always leads to turmoil. Self-talk, which is complete, leads to freedom.** As long as something remains incomplete (this may be related to work or anything else), the subconscious mind does not feel contented, and this state of discontentment leads to discomfort.

There is another example that illustrates this point in a different way. Mr. Sharma was in a lot of discomfort one evening. His wife noticed that his mind was not in the present. He was not able to focus on his food, neither was he able to enjoy watching the television. He could not even sleep. He was twisting and turning in bed. His wife finally asked him, "What is it that is making you so restless?" Mr. Sharma sat up and replied, "I am extremely anxious. I had borrowed some money from Mr. Verma and assured him that I would return it tomorrow morning at ten." His wife retorted, "So what? Return it!" He lamented, "I can't. I don't have the requisite amount of money. Mr. Verma called up in the afternoon to remind me about returning the money by tomorrow morning and said he would be waiting for me. I wanted to say 'no' but a 'yes' slipped out of my mouth. Now I must muster the money some way or the other."

His wife was listening silently. She then smiled and said, "Just give me Mr. Verma's phone number."

She took the number and called up Mr. Verma. She spoke calmly, "Mr. Verma, my husband had promised that he would return your money tomorrow morning, but unfortunately he does not have the requisite funds today. When he has enough money, he will definitely call you up and repay you. Thank you!" She placed the telephone handset on its cradle.

Mr. Sharma was listening to his wife. His face lit up with relief and he went to sleep peacefully. He immediately slipped into deep sleep. However, on the other side, Mr. Verma lost his sleep. Now he was troubled by the following self-talk: "He's not returning the money. How should I confront him? How will I get back my money? How will I arrange for money?" On one side, the self-talk of one person was taken to completion and he attained peace. However, on the other side, the negative self-talk of the other person had just begun. Now, until the self-talk is not taken to its completion, it will continue.

If you give completion to your self-talk you will save a lot of time and also raise your efficiency. Till the time you are not free from negative self-talk, you will remain distressed and will not be able to focus on the job at hand. You will not be able to relax. There are many people who are trapped in this state for their entire day.

Thus, through his week-long experiment, Mr. Macey inculcated the habit of completing his self-talk in his routine matters. In situations where he used to spend hours in useless self-talk, he began to wind it up in minutes.

As Mr. Macey worked on his first ten minutes systematically, all his decisions and tasks during the whole day lined up right. His self-talk became organized, disciplined and well-directed. He started writing down his weekly schedule. He jotted down his major tasks on the white board. At home, he decided in advance when to bathe, which clothes to wear, which papers and files to carry to office, etc. Thus, around 40-50% of his futile self-talk was eliminated. Mr. Macey now transformed into an efficient manager like Mr. Spick.

With every breath I am receiving the goodness and grace of life.

18
Captive Or Free

Aniket (name changed) came to the Satsang to share an incident which was troubling him since many years. Anguish was written all over his face.

"Speak out your heart openly without any qualms, Aniket."

Breathing deeply Aniket began, "Sirshree, this was about ten years ago… After my father's demise, the very people whom I trusted the most stabbed me in the back. I have no complaints about outsiders… they are after all, outsiders. As he continued, tears welled up in his eyes. But my own kith and kin have behaved so badly with me that I can never ever forgive them. I feel agitated at their mere sight. Sometimes I get mad… so much so that I feel like committing suicide or even finishing them off!"

Aniket looked at Sirshree with tearful eyes,

"Sirshree, my father died twelve years ago, when I was seventeen. I was in the city for studies when this unfortunate event occurred. Due to my father's unexpected demise, I could not even return home to catch a last glimpse of him. I had to continue my further studies in the city. After spending a couple of days in my village, I returned to my college. Now my elder brother was our only support. I was studying and my sister was already married.

I was studying in the 12th grade and the final exams were impending. I managed to steady myself by setting the target of fulfilling my father's dream of scoring a very good percentage in the exams. Driven by the hope of fulfilling my father's wishes, I immersed myself into my studies. I did extremely well in the examinations, securing a very high percentage. I managed to gain admission for medical studies at the university. I had a week to pay my course fees. I was dancing with joy when I reached my village. When my mother heard about the prospect of her son becoming a doctor, she was ecstatic!" Aniket's eyes were gleaming as he said this.

"My elder brother was also happy for me . After dinner, I informed my brother that I had to pay twelve thousand rupees for the first term of the course and three thousand for the hostel accommodation. On hearing this, there was a stark change in my brother's demeanour.

'Where will we get so much money from?' he said vehemently. 'I don't have anything.' He got up and left. But I remained calm.

The next day I asked my brother in his wife's presence, can we sell half the plot of land that we have inherited after father's death? When I become a doctor, we shall be able to buy it back.

'*Your* plot of land?! Which land?' my brother started laughing derisively.

"You may keep your share with you, I told my brother, but give me the documents for my share of the land so that I can sell it for paying my fees.

'Land!? What land?' shouted my brother, 'There's nothing in your name now.' He laid out some legal papers before me and said, 'Read it yourself.'

"When I saw the legal document, I recalled at once that two months after my father's demise, my brother had called me over to the village for some urgent work. I had then signed on these papers wherever he had asked me to, without getting into its content, trusting him fully.

"That was the worst shock of my life, Sirshree. My own brother had duped me and snatched away my land. I could not believe what he had done to me. I could not bear this shock. I headed straight for the river. I considered committing suicide, but after some time I managed to muster some patience and returned home.

In the evening I went to my brother again and said, 'keep all you want, but please lend me some money for my studies. I assure you that I will return all your money.'

"My brother turned a deaf ear to my plea and walked out. I got the answer. I understood what it meant. It was of no use talking to such stone-hearted people. Reminiscing about my father, I wept all night.

I then decided to request with my professor. The next day I went to the city and related the entire story to my professor. I beseeched him, 'If you help me, I will always be indebted to you. I will return your money as soon as possible.'

"But fortune deserted me there too. My teacher nonchalantly dismissed me saying, 'I cannot do anything for you. If you do not have the money, I have no choice but to deny your admission to the course.' And he signed to that effect on my file.

"These two signatures have literally ruined my life. I could see my father's dream crumbling down before my eyes, but what could I do? I resolved to put aside my misfortune and moved to another town to start a small business. I did quite well. I achieved success in my venture. My efforts yielded a lot of money in a short time.

"I am now settled and satisfied from the financial perspective. However, I simply cannot forget the damage that my brother has inflicted on my life. Recently I had been to my village. Burying the bad memories, I even helped my brother by lending him some money. But I am unable to erase that day, that situation, that bleakest moment of my life from my mind.

"Everything is fine now, but whenever I catch a glimpse of the doctor who lives just across my house, I start squirming with uneasiness. My mind replays the entire sequence of events. I still spend sleepless nights recalling how my brother usurped my property.

"Why does this happen? Tell me Sirshree, what should I do? If my mind continues with these thoughts, I will surely go crazy. I am already on sleeping pills now. I always feel despondent about the fact that I could not fulfil my father's dream. Had my brother or teacher helped me then, I would definitely have gone places. I would have been so happy to be a doctor. Where is my fault in all that has happened? Why am I going through such an ordeal?"

Aniket started weeping. His face was writ with mixed feelings of anger and grief.

"You have gone through a lot of pain." Said Sirshree. "No brother should ever behave that way. You are right, there is no fault of yours in all this. But just think, what kind of life do you want to lead – captive or free?"

Aniket was taken by surprise and looked up.

Sirshree took out a book which contained several stories. Pointing to one of the stories, Sirshree suggested Aniket to read the story and then talk further.

Looking at the book Aniket asked, "Sirshree, what captivity are you talking about?"

"First read the story, you will come to know", said Sirshree.

The story was as follows:

There were two friends, Manjeet and Rakesh, who happened to meet each other while shopping. Rakesh called out, "Hey Manjeet! What are you doing here?!"

Manjeet looked up, startled, and replied, "Hi Rakesh! Good to see you!" They hugged each other warmly.

Rakesh said, "I live right down this street. Come… let's go to my place and chat."

Manjeet agreed and both of them walked towards Rakesh's house. They filled in about themselves to each other.

"Manjeet, I think about you every day," said Rakesh.

"Oh! Do you?! How?" wondered Manjeet.

"Come on Manjeet, have you forgotten? I still remember each day that we spent together as prisoners of war."

"Oh yes! We were together in the enemy prison. I had really forgotten that," said Manjeet.

"How on earth can you forget that?" countered Rakesh with a perplexed look on his face. "I cannot but recall every day that we spent in jail. It is now eleven years since that episode. We were captured by the enemy during the war and held as prisoners. We were tortured so gruesomely in the enemy camp! We were starved in their jails. All they fed us was one dry piece of bread. On one occasion, for no reason they forced you to go without food for three days. They made us fill up a dried lake so as to convert it into a sports ground. They abused and tortured us callously without any reason. I remember each and every day…" Manjeet could see the agony in Rakesh's eyes.

"Oh, yes. We did go through all that in the jail."

"Manjeet, how can you forget so easily?" asked a shocked Rakesh. "I remember each moment. They made us run ten laps around the same ground that we had built. It was no different from hell!"

"Rakesh, you *still* remember all those details?" Manjeet was astounded.

"Yes, I still remember everything." Rakesh's gaze drifted up into the sky, lost in his memories. "Every night, when I lie down to sleep, I remember the bristly blanket I used to wrap around and the rocky surface on which I slept. I feel the same discomfort even today. In the last few years there has not been a single moment that I was free from these memories. I can always see the jailor and his henchmen very clearly. I get nightmares about our life in jail all the time."

"This means that you are still a captive in prison," stated Manjeet calmly. "You may be physically out of jail, but your mind is still in the prison. You are suffering the same misery even now. Your prison term is still going on. They had held us captive only for a year, after which I became free. But you are not yet freed. Till the time you hold on to these forlorn thoughts, your imprisonment will go on."

As the narrative ended, Aniket shut his eyes. His face loosened up and the lines of agony began to fade. He opened his eyes with calmness and smiled, "Sirshree, I have understood… I have got my answer." Aniket's eyes reflected the happiness of having found the solution to his predicament.

"Sirshree, thank you very much! My gratitude unto you! Today, I am experiencing the joy of freedom after reading this story. Till today, I was living my life like Rakesh. Henceforth I will live like Manjeet. I will not stay in prison any longer. I have understood that the cause of my suffering was not those people, but myself. Henceforth, after each incident, I will ask myself the question that you had asked me in the beginning, 'What kind of life do you want to lead – captive or free?' Sirshree, this is not a question, rather it is a *mantra* for freedom."

It is our own self-talk that locks us up in prison, but the same self-talk can liberate us from prison too. The moment the efficacy of self-talk is understood, a person who is locked up in prison will instantly find himself liberated. If it is not understood, even the judge who sentences people into imprisonment will walk into his own prison!

Love heals diseases... I love everyone.
I forgive everyone...And so does everyone forgive
me...I am God's child.

SECTION IV
HOW THE MAGIC OF SELF-TALK WORKS IN NATURE THROUGH SILENCE

All miracles happening on Earth
happen on the basis of our power of faith.
We obtain proofs for the faith we have.
Therefore, to live a Supreme Life,
start believing in positive self-talk
from now on which will make your beliefs
positive and beneficial for you
as well as others.

19
Self-talk Is Self-Reporting

Until today if anyone gave you a negative reaction to any of your actions, you most probably spoke ill of him and said, "This person causes pain to me, he hurts my feelings." However, from today onwards, you do not have to say that. What the world says about you is not important. What is most important is what you tell yourself about yourself. Give yourself information about, "What am I telling myself about myself?" In this way, give yourself your report.

If all day long somebody made you unhappy or gave you a response that hurt you, your self-talk may have been, "This person has spoilt my day... he has upset me..." But from now onwards you do not have to say that. Whenever you experience such an incident which makes you unhappy, you have to say to yourself, "Change the reporting." This technique is a very important one and is called 'self-reporting'.

Let us understand how you have to report to yourself. If a person hurts you or makes you unhappy, say to yourself, "Due to such a response from this person, I allowed myself to become unhappy." For example, if you are sitting in your room along with your friend and he just gets up and leaves without saying anything to you, you would normally be upset with him. But henceforth in such a situation you have to say, "My friend left without saying anything to me; so I allowed myself to get upset. I allowed my day to get spoilt due to vexation. I am ruining my day due to this vexation."

Self-reporting in this manner will create miracles in your life. You will stop getting distressed at small matters in your life. By persisting with this experiment, you will not feel an iota of unhappiness in bigger incidents too. Sometimes during sickness, you might feel pain, but you will not grieve due to the pain. Such a life is a Supreme Life. As soon as you change your self-talk (self-reporting), your sorrow and misery vanishes. Until now, some events made you sad, but henceforth after changing your self-reporting, you will not feel sad. Even if something is happening against your wishes, you will observe that you are not feeling sad. You will be surprised. Never say, "I am sad." Always say, **"I am allowing myself to feel sad, I am allowing myself to get bored. Who else can dare to make me sad?"** If you change your self-talk and flip your self-reporting around, you will be amazed to find that nobody is capable of making you sad.

People become very unhappy upon listening to criticism or abusive words. If faced with such a situation, you should tell yourself, "Canes and stones can break my bones but words can never break my bones. I am allowing myself to become unhappy on listening to people criticizing me." Report to yourself in this manner. When you report this kind of news to yourself, *you* become responsible for your unhappiness. When you become responsible for your unhappiness, you stop complaining about others. **You will then gain the insight that if it is you who allows yourself to become unhappy, then you can also allow yourself to become happy.** Thus a new understanding will be born. You can then resolve to remain happy always. This fifth step for a Supreme Life is crucial.

Break free out of the mesh of your usual old self-talk. Refresh your self-talk with new words and new style. Otherwise you will continue to get depressed at ill-disposed reactions from people and say, "I am depressed." Turn around the report you give yourself and say, "I am allowing myself to get depressed." By saying so you will not feel depressed, instead you will light the lamp of a new hope. Whenever you feel bored, never say, "I am bored." Your self-reporting should be, "I am allowing myself to be bored due to circumstances" or else, "I am allowing myself to be bored because I don't have a resolute aim." Such reporting will bestow a new understanding upon you.

If you experiment with this right from today, you will see that sorrow will never be able to sadden you and hopelessness will never be able to make you feel hopeless. Whenever you feel sad or hopeless, assess your self-talk and check whether you are really sad or hopeless or you are allowing yourself to become sad or hopeless.

Upon changing your self-talk you will instantly feel happy, because saying to yourself, "I am allowing myself to become sad" obliterates the sadness and hurt. In this way, change your self-talk during any difficulty you face in life. You have to become a good-news reporter and give your report to yourself every single day. If you become a good-news reporter to yourself, you will become so for others as well.

With the help of the examples you have read so far, you have learnt the art of self-talk (or self-reporting). Make a decision now to observe proper self-talk every day. The magic of self-talk will make your life supreme.

20

Convert Sadness Into Happiness Through Self-talk

Every moment, every day, various incidents take place all around you. During or after those incidents, you either feel good or you feel bad.

We all want to feel good inside. Now the question arises, how do we feel good every day, in every incident? So come, let us work on this and shed some light on it, due to which your life will become the best and your attitude will change for the better.

Ask yourself the question, where is it that you feel good or bad upon experiencing a good or bad event? Is it in your body or in your neighbour's body? If it is in your neighbour's body, you cannot do anything about it. If it is in your body, who is responsible for it? If that feeling has to be changed, who is going to come and change it? The Prime Minister? Or you yourself?

When you ask yourself the above questions, you will come to know that:

1. Every feeling is felt by us in *our* body.
2. We are responsible for experiencing that feeling, and not our neighbour or this world.

3. If bad feelings are to be changed, nobody but you yourself have to change it.

4. If you have understood all this, how are you feeling right now? Are you feeling what you want to, or something else?

5. If you are feeling bad, are you ready to change that feeling? "Yes!"

6. If 'yes', when? "Here and now!"

7. How will you change it? "By changing your self-talk."

You do not require much time to change your feelings. If you wish, you can change them in an instant, which will transform your self-talk into positive self-talk. If you consider your feelings of sorrow to be a consequence of somebody else's behaviour, rest assured that you will never be happy because every person's attitude and thinking pattern is different.

Henceforth, at every moment and during every event, ask yourself the question, "How am I feeling right now? If I am feeling bad, who is responsible for it? Who will change this feeling? When and how?" You will then witness that you feel happy after changing your self-talk and the person responsible for it will be none other than you.

Now let us see how the thinking pattern works differently in different people. There are as many different worlds as there are people, because each one sees this world from their own point of view. The viewpoint of each person creates a structure (thinking pattern, map) in his brain. It is this pattern that becomes the cause of happiness and sadness. Every person is right according to the frame of his own world, i.e. whatever is said by any person is right as per his understanding. Everybody has a structure or pattern in his mind about his life and his world and it is according to this pattern that he says and does things. Others might feel that he is wrong in what he is saying and doing but when they understand the reason behind his words and actions, the misunderstanding clears up.

Everybody is right as per their thinking pattern

Every person has his own existence and his own world. There is a distinct frame of his world through which he sees, but we cannot see his frame. We often wonder, 'Why is he speaking this way…? Why does this person behave this way…? Why is this person so timid…?' But from today onwards, **we do not have to look at how others are at fault, we have to look at how they are right.** Everybody is right, whoever it may be. Even a criminal is right because his world too has a structure or pattern. He sees as per his thinking pattern. We will understand this with the help of an example, so that our relations with people will improve.

When you stroll on the terrace of your building in the evening you see a lot of birds, the clouds, the setting sun, etc. This is what you see. Have you ever wondered how birds look at the world? How do the birds flying in the sky look below? Think from their point of view. How does the world appear to them? If they had the ability to think, what would they think? When we look at the birds, what are the things that we can think of? We can think that we look up at the sky and are able to see the stars and the moon; if birds were to fly with their faces facing the sky, they too would be able to see the sky as we do. But at present they do not see the way we see. How would we be appearing to them? If they could think, what would they be thinking?

If we look through the eyes of birds, we will be able to understand their view. If birds could tell us their perspective they would say, "People walk on the ground upside down. When they have built tall buildings, they should at least walk on the terrace. In spite of so much development and progress they still walk on the ground. People should not sit confined in closed boxes [buildings, houses]. Only some children take time out to come on the terrace and look at the sky." This is what the birds see and they too are right. What man thinks of birds is also right as per his perspective. Everybody is right as per their thinking pattern.

How have we looked at life till today? We have looked at it as per our thinking pattern. Till the time we keep looking through frames or patterns, we will not achieve Supreme Life. Today if you look at the thinking pattern of two people regarding how they perceive the world, it would be different from each other. Everybody has his own world, his own dreams. There is only one state (that of self-realization) where the thinking patterns of some people become the same because all old patterns and moulds fall apart. These people break out of limitations and become 'unlimited' and become stabilized in the present from being in the past and the future.

Break your thinking pattern

What is happening in the present is the truth. What has happened is in our memory. What is going to happen is a figment of our imagination. The truth is 'now' – if you start your journey from this truth you can reach the Supreme State. To reach that Supreme State start seeing with the right viewpoint and be honest in your self-talk.

This is the first condition – you have to talk honestly with yourself without hiding your reality. Ask yourself, **"According to my thinking pattern, this seems to be wrong; is it really wrong or is my thought pattern showing it to be wrong?"** When you ask yourself this question honestly, you will find the right answers inside yourself.

There was a person who was habituated to negative self-talk. All the people around him appeared to be emissaries of Satan to him. His self-talk made him believe so. People carry their own perceptions about the world and say, "I was walking along the street and this person looked at me in such a way, he definitely must be thinking something malicious about me." In this way he concocts an imaginary story and lives on that basis. One day he realizes that none of his beliefs were true. All the stories he made up right from childhood to old age and all his self-talks bore no semblance of truth.

Why then was this person scared? He was scared because he had thought and decided that 'all the people around me are sinister and cruel.' He felt so biased on his thinking pattern and he was thus leading a fearful life.

If you live boldly without a trace of fear, the thinking pattern with which you look at the world will be totally different. This state is achieved gradually because we have to get rid of all apprehensions and fears and reach the Supreme State of Supreme Consciousness and eternal bliss. With self-talk, we can instantly switch our state in the present.

You should give your body some self-suggestions such as, *"I am health."* This self-talk has a positive effect on you because whatever is appended to 'I am' becomes true. You can also recite the phrase, *"God cannot fall sick, therefore I too cannot fall sick."* This self-talk sustains truth; it is magical. These phrases have the desired effect because there is positive energy in the truth.

When the truth is recited, it has instant effect because upon just hearing the above health related self-suggestion, positive vibrations are produced inside you. When a sick person reiterates that God cannot fall ill, his faith begins to show results. All the miracles that happen on Earth are based on the power of our faith. **As our conviction, so are the proofs that we get.** Hence to attain a Supreme Life keep faith on positive self-talk. Do not fear the cat cutting across your path, the lightning striking across the sky, the wrong planetary positions or the wailing of dogs. Always keep faith that you are born to do great work.

Know all these facts and break your thinking pattern. Experience what you want to experience. Every day, after every incident, carry out this self-talk: "How am I feeling right now?" If the answer is "bad", ask yourself, "Where am I experiencing this feeling?" We experience every feeling inside our body. Then ask, "Who is responsible for experiencing this feeling?" Give yourself the answer, "It's me who is responsible, and not the incident." Then ask yourself, "Can I change this feeling if I want to?" Yes, if you want to, you can change the feeling. "Can I change this feeling right now?" Yes, you can change your feelings, thoughts, speech and actions whenever you want to. At the end, ask yourself the important question, "How can I change this feeling?" You know the answer by now! "Through self-talk." You will instantly feel better.

I care my experiences with love, happiness and ease.
There is magic in my hands and self-talk.

21

How To Communicate With Nature In Silence

Just like the sea is the source of the river, similarly Silence (*moun*) is the source of speech. Like the river journeys to meet the sea, similarly man journeys within himself to meet Silence. This journey is a good *karma* (deed). Idling away in laziness and being seated in the experience of Silence are two different things. The outcome of sitting in laziness is negative while the outcome of spending a few moments in Silence is positive.

Without the paper, the words written on it are in vain. Similarly, speech without Silence is in vain. There is silence between every two words. There is silence behind each word too. **Realizing and experiencing Silence is the junction in the journey towards Supreme Life.** The new track of Self Expression (expression of the true universal self through our body) originates from this junction. Until man reaches the junction of Silence, he just 'works' in his life. After arriving at the junction of Silence, man never 'works' because his work now turns into Self Expression, devotion and impersonal service (*seva*).

We must take some time out every day to quieten down the body and mind. By sitting in Silence, you will uncover many facts about yourself. Man bonds with others through the means of talk, while he contacts himself through self-talk. He connects with the Almighty through prayer. He connects with his Self through silence and gets stabilized in his Self. This step is essential for one to know his true Self (Self Realization) and to live a Supreme Life.

Life, Living being and Consciousness

You must have seen a burning incense stick. There is a thin wooden stick inside it; that stick can be considered to symbolize 'a living being' (*jeev*). If there is no incense applied on the stick, you would say that it is of no use. If an infant does not cry upon birth, its parents have to cry, because the crying of the infant indicates that it is alive. Therefore, when the infant lets out a cry, its parents smile. Just like life without breath is useless, similarly life without Silence is useless. Silence is a vital element of our life.

An incense stick symbolizes a living being and the incense applied on it symbolizes 'life' (*jeevan*). The incense of 'age' is applied on every person's life. In some, this incense sustains for sixty years while it sustains for eighty years or a hundred years in some others. The incense stick burns until the incense lasts. This is how life is.

The burning part of the incense stick is '*jeevatma*'. *Jeevatma* means Consciousness, the living presence, which is within all of us, without which life has no significance. It is due to this consciousness that life functions. It is due to the burning part at the tip that the incense stick gives out fragrance. Similarly, it is due to Consciousness that the body performs its deeds (*karma*). The Consciousness slowly erodes away the body (incense stick) and reveals itself in the process. The Consciousness enlivens the body and is slowly expressing itself, asserting its existence (spreading fragrance).

The ash of the mind and the smoke of thoughts

The Consciousness inside us (the burning part of an incense stick) has got covered by ash. The ash symbolizes the contrast mind. To uncover the Consciousness, we need to blow aside the ash through our self-talk. We have to re-awaken the Consciousness. When ash falls off an incense stick, smoke is also emanated. That smoke stinks due to thoughts of lust, anger, fear, greed, attachment, hatred and ego.

Several kinds of thoughts run in one's mind from morning to night. These thoughts stink of worry and fear. Worry is such a thing that kills you slowly all your life. We all know about fear. People fear things like, 'What will happen tomorrow… what if I am fired from my job… what will happen to me when I grow old… what will happen of me after my kids marry…' This way, there are many fears that reside in man's mind. Due to these fears man dies every moment every day. These fears create misery in him, i.e. the smoke stinks of sadness. When one thought ceases, another one arises. As one sorrow ends, thought of another sorrow begins. This creates a vicious cycle of misery. As one misery ends, a second one starts. As the second one ends, a third one starts. This cycle never ends.

When our happiness lies in the past or in the future, we are not able to be happy in the present. People say, "I will be happy when I am promoted" or "I will be happy on my birthday." However, they do not know that this is false happiness which depends on reasons. Reasons may be there today, but tomorrow they may vanish. True happiness is in the present, without any reason, here and now. The present, in itself is complete happiness. The knack of being happy in the present is essential in order to attain Supreme Life. The mind will always keep running into the future or into the past but now it needs to be trained to remain in the present.

Within every living being there is life (Consciousness, Self). Likewise, there is life within you. You too can sing out in happiness like the birds, but you have misunderstood what life is all about. 'Life means everyday drudgeries' is what many think of life, but that is not life.

Life is the Consciousness, the Self inside us. Stabilizing yourself in that Consciousness and utilizing your body for the expression of the Self is the ultimate aim of Supreme Life. After stabilizing in that Consciousness you will experience that live entity within yourself and you will say, *"I am happy because I am. I am happy because of my existence. I don't need any other reason to be happy."* If you truly experience Life within yourself, you will not need any other kind of happiness. You will get unlimited external joys in your life but they will just be a bonus for you because true happiness is in the Experience of Being and its Expression.

You will succeed in business; you will celebrate your birthday with your family... all these things will go on. But when you will attain true happiness after achieving the Supreme Life (stabilization in the Consciousness or Self), you will not be dependent on external pleasures. Today people do not know true happiness and are therefore dependent on external pleasures. Man fears death and indulges in self-talk like, "My relative brings me joy and happiness, what will happen of me if he dies? My boss can give me a promotion, what will happen if he goes away somewhere?" In this way man lives an anxious life due to wrong self-talk. A life full of doubt and anxiety cannot become a supreme life. You have to liberate yourself from such negative self-talk and understand that the same life which is functioning within your relative or boss is chirping in you too.

The self-talk "life is difficult" is inappropriate. If one keeps repeating this dialogue within himself, if he believes in this notion, he will get proofs of the same, which will validate his belief further. The negative self-talk "life is difficult" will start working in his life and make his life difficult to live. This is nature's law – 'What you believe is what you will get.' The self-talk inside a person leading a Supreme Life is: *"Life is beautiful, life is courage, life is zest, life is self-expression."* When life awakens in birds every morning, it takes the form of a melodious tune and starts chirping. It is this same life in flowers that takes the form of color and fragrance and spreads all around. Life flows in the rippling streams. Life presents various amazing scenes every day in the sky in the form of clouds and the sun. Looking at it, your life becomes cheerful in addition to becoming simple. The truth is that life is happiness, life is love, life is God.

You all must have seen a cuckoo cooing and a nightingale singing but have you ever sensed the life gushing inside them? These birds chirp because there is a live Consciousness inside them. That Consciousness is such that it gives them boundless joy and spurs them to sing. The same Consciousness is present inside us too but we are not able to sing, and live our lives in sorrow, because our Consciousness is covered by the ash of the contrast mind. Clearing aside that ash is the first objective of life.

Whenever you see expressions of happiness in birds, flowers and children, carry out this self-talk:

"The life, which is expressing itself and dancing in these birds, flowers and children, is present in me too. It is due to the indolence (lethargy) of my body that the life inside me is not being able to celebrate. Therefore, I must eradicate this indolence from my body. I heartily thank these birds, flowers, clouds, hills, streams, trees and children for reminding me of the life present inside me. I will now see the life in people and not focus on their body. I will always remember Life and live a Supreme Life."

With this self-talk you will experience the zest of Supreme Life. With this self-talk you will fall in love with life. What you focus on is what you become. This is the rule of nature. By focusing on life in this manner, you will yourself become Life. This is not the art of living, but the art of being life. To learn the art of being life or leading a Supreme Life, you have to learn the magic of self-talk. You have to learn to keep the remote control of your life firmly in your own hands. When you resort to positive self-talk with awareness and understanding, you are saved from a lot of sorrows and you become capable of dissolving the ones that have come your way.

The day your negative self-talk fades away from your life, you will say, "*The aim of life is life itself, life is in the present.*" With this self-talk you will sow the seed of Supreme Life in the field of the present.

Whenever sadness and hopelessness loom over you, carry out the following self-talk:

"*Life is a spark; the contrast mind is the ash covering the spark.*

The past is gone, the future is yet to come,

the present is 'now' and is the truth,

therefore, the present is my life.

True happiness is in the present, here and now.

The present in itself is complete happiness."

God has created everything in abundance but we always find everything lacking. If the borders between countries are erased, you will find that everything is abundant. We have to erase the lines dividing every country and every farm. After that you will say, "*Food, water, money, love, time and life are abundant; nothing is lacking.*" To believe in this self-talk you need to know the secret of Supreme Life.

Your disbelief reduces your faith and that is why you wish to give out less time, less money or less love to others. In ignorance, man always repeats the following self-talk:

- "If I give someone my time, money or love, there will be very little or none left for me."

- "There is less love, money, time, happiness, health and contentment."

- "By giving it decreases, by taking it increases, my wealth will increase only if someone else's decreases."
- "Only if something is snatched away from someone will someone else get it."

The above-mentioned self-talk that goes on due to ignorance has become imprinted in man's mind, due to which he spares very little for others.

The day your self-talk is enriched with faith and knowledge, the dialogues within you will be:

- "God has created everything in abundance."
- "Time, money, love, health, happiness and life are abundant."
- "When we give things to others, we progress. When we take things from others, we merely survive."

When you start believing in this self-talk you will not hesitate to give others time, money or love. Then you will see all these things increasing in your life. If today you flip your self-talk from "money is less" and start believing that "money, love, happiness and life grow quite easily", you will find that the flow of money, love and happiness is occurring easily in your life. You will definitely get proofs for it.

SECTION V
LEARN THE MAGIC OF SELF-TALK

To become life
and to learn the art of leading
a supreme life,
you need to learn the magic of self-talk.
With full awareness
and with the right understanding,
when you engage in positive self-talk,
you save yourself from various miseries
and become capable of
dissolving those sorrows
which have already appeared in
your life.

22

How To Carry Out Self-talk

When man's thoughts are not aligned with the Supreme Power running this world, he is plagued with many difficulties. Whenever you are troubled by physical, mental, social or financial difficulties, repeat the following self-talk to yourself until you feel strong enough to resolve those difficulties: *"What are the thoughts inside me due to which I am suffering from this problem? I am now ready to let go of that thought pattern which has created this problem."*

"My new thought pattern would now be that of health, contentment and prosperity, which I will repeat again and again." To lead a Supreme life, make this your new thought pattern and repeat it as frequently as possible and imagine that you are going through the process of getting well and making great progress.

When you are feeling anxious and doubts surmount you, repeat the following self-dialogue until you feel alleviated: *"I have faith in life; therefore, fear and insecurity are merely thoughts that come and go. I am secure."*

Cancel Cancel Cancel

Whenever you fear any calamity or a negative thought appears in your mind, say the following to yourself three times to wipe out its effect – "Cancel, Cancel, Cancel." Then say, *"The past is gone, the storm has subsided, hence I am at peace. I am inspecting the self-talk that has created this fear. I have cancelled that self-talk three times (Cancel, Cancel, Cancel). Now this self-talk will not be repeated by me even unconsciously."*

Let desires not become a disease

The pain that arises in your body becomes a sorrow. Many a time man's intense desire becomes a disease. In such a state, reiterate the self-dialogue – *"I am worthy of love, I love and accept myself."*

Low self esteem

When your mind feels low on self-esteem or develops an inferiority complex, hammer in the following self-talk time and again:

1. *"I am the Divine expression of Life. I have understood how important and extraordinary I am."*

2. *"I love, respect and care for my body, mind, intellect and feelings."*

Let old age not become an ailment

People who fall victim to negative thoughts due to old age, should carry out the self-talk given below several times a day:

1. *"Every stage of life is special; I love and accept myself at every stage of my life."*

2. *"I forgive and release my past, I am moving ahead to attain freedom in the present and eternal bliss in the future."*

3. *"Life loves me, I am strong and capable, I am part of the Universe, therefore I love myself in every state."*

4. *"I am completely balanced. In every stage of life, I progress ahead with ease and happiness."*

Improve your human relations with self-talk

Some people do not find themselves very good at interacting with others. They are not able to make friends easily. Abolish this deficiency with the following self-dialogues:

1. *"Everybody is good and friendly to me. I am well tuned with the highest way of life."*

2. *"I look at all my experiences with love, I also look at others with bright love."*

3. *"Each and every person perceives me positively. I receive a lot of appreciation and love."*

Especially for women

Very often, women face difficulties due to their body, or they suffer from very low self-esteem and consider themselves weak. The self-verbalization given below can help you accept your body:

1. *"I am happy with what I am. I accept my body as it is, because my body is my friend."*

2. *"It is a unique experience to be a woman. I am becoming aware of all my capabilities and I also accept all my limitations. I am always secure and full of love."*

Self-talk to take up responsibilities

Some people want to be successful but fear the responsibilities that come along with success. This fear often makes them fall ill frequently so that they can escape from taking up responsibilities. Similarly, children often fall sick before their exams. During such times, restate the following every day:

1. *"Being successful is safe for me, Life loves me and therefore wants to see me successful."*

2. *"It is only me who thinks for me. I always keep my thinking high."*

Freedom from self-hatred with the help of self-talk

Due to guilt some people are not able to accept themselves, they also keep punishing themselves. Many a time the feeling of guilt may manifest in the form of illnesses. In such circumstances one needs to hammer in the following self-talk repeatedly:

1. *"I have every right to be happy in life, I am open to receive all the happiness that life offers."*
2. *"Everything happening in my life is good and right as per the divine plan."*
3. *"I choose to be happy, I choose to accept the way I am."*
4. *"I am releasing easily all that is not necessary for me now. It is right to cast aside all my false beliefs. The disease that I do not need is leaving my body."*
5. *"I forgive myself with love and understanding, now I am free, I am freedom."*
6. *"I am in harmony with supreme life. I am not a victim of any guilt."*

Increase your self-confidence through self-talk

Due to fear, people lose their self-confidence. They live a constricted life. If you are in such a state, repeat any one of the following lines every morning:

1. *"I am opening myself to life, I am eager to experience life."*
2. *"I am God's property, only faith can touch me."*
3. *"I am love, I am goodness, I wish to happily let my life flow."*

4. *"I allow myself to progress ahead. It is always safe to progress."*

Talk about your feelings and remain free from illnesses.

Some people find it difficult to express their thoughts, opinions and feelings. Such people are likely to develop diseases involving the throat and lungs. To prevent such problems (diseases), drill in the following self-suggestions whenever you can:

1. *"I know that life is on my side. Whoever I need, I always get."*
2. *"I express my feelings. Expressing feelings is always safe for me."*
3. *"I am free to ask for whatever I need. It is safe to put myself forward."*
4. *"I speak for my rights effortlessly."*
5. *"I communicate with everyone happily, peacefully, courageously and with an open heart."*
6. *"I am free of all blame; I pay attention to others' point of view. I open my heart and sing songs of love. I can speak for myself with ease. I feel comfortable while expressing my feelings."*

Do not fear mistakes, take the help of self-talk

Some people do not even begin any new task due to fear of committing mistakes. They should repeat this self-dialogue: "*I need to go through various kinds of experiences in order to grow. I forgive all my mistakes. I love myself, life also loves me, I will always continue to love myself.*"

How to guard against loneliness and allergies

Some people are calm and pleasant when they are alone, but when they are amidst people, they fall a victim to skin diseases, allergies and loneliness. The self-dialogues given below will help such people:

1. *"I am free from all irritation. I am capable of pacifying my thoughts."*

2. *"I believe that whatever is happening in my life is according to the divine plan. I am at ease."*

3. *"I accept myself as I am and I also allow others to remain as they are."*

Let desires not become disease, prepare to leave behind the old and to change

Some people are not able to accept changes. They get perturbed even by weather changes. They fall sick in a new atmosphere. Such people have a tendency of accumulating things. A lot of stomach ailments develop due to such tendencies. In case you experience such problems, the self-talk that will benefit you is:

1. *"I am clear in my understanding and I am willing to change with time. I relinquish the old and welcome the new easily and happily."*

2. *"I am the one who operates my mind. It is easy to bring my mind into a new mould of thinking. I am letting go of my old fixed pattern of thinking."*

3. *"I am fine at all times. I have empathy for myself and for others. Everything is excellent."*

4. *"I let go of all those thoughts that impede my progress and stop me from being what I want to be. I release all such thoughts.'*

5. *"I am now absolutely ready to change myself."*

Ask for your rights and remain healthy

Some people are not able to speak up for their rights. Such people always face inconveniences at all places. They keep fretting within themselves and thus invite a lot many ailments. In case you are one of them, the following self-dialogue will open you up:

1. *"It is my birth right to live a full, straightforward and easy life. I now choose to live life to its fullest."*

2. *"I have every right to feel good. I create only peace and goodwill within me and around me. I am filling my world with happiness."*

Break your patterns through acceptance and flexibility in thinking

Some people are just not willing to change their way of thinking; their intellect is not flexible. They are not able to accept the new easily. Repeating the following self-talk will prove to be very beneficial for them:

1. *"I am ready for the grand experiences of life and I embrace each of my experiences to my heart."* By repeating this self-dialogue every day, they can break their thinking pattern. Or they can also repeat: *"I am open to receive divine guidance, I am ready to let go of my old pattern of thinking. God is guiding me towards achieving the highest fulfilment. I thank God for His grace."*

2. *"I am able to keep control over my thoughts at all times. Thoughts are my slaves, I am not under their obligation, I am a clear thinker."*

3. *"I look at all aspects easily and with flexibility. Everything, every task, every work has various aspects. I am open."*

4. *"In spite of flexibility in my thinking, I am safe."*

Praise yourself, avoid self-depreciation

There are also some people in this world who do not want to listen to their praise. They are always engaged in self-depreciation. Due to this, they are unable to praise others too. If you are a victim of such misapprehension, the self-dialogues given below will liberate you from it:

1. *"I am allowing myself to be all that I can be. I also give others this right. I love them and praise them."*
2. *"I create only happy feelings around me. I am surrounded with love and only love."*

The secret of liberation from the past

Some people like to live in their past. They are always reminiscing sad old memories and are lost in them, so much so that it becomes a habit for them. They are unable to shift their attention to anything else. The self-talk given below can help them immensely:

1. *"I permit time to heal my wounds. I am now ready to welcome each and every new moment."*
2. *"I am enthusiastic and eager to change myself and to move ahead and create a new future."*
3. *"I keep my mind and body balanced at all times. I now choose only those thoughts that make me feel good."*
4. *"I easily forget all the problems of the past. I am opening myself to receive a bright future. There are endless opportunities for me to change and progress in every aspect."*

To achieve progress, respect yourself

Apart from respecting others, respect yourself too. This is not ego but understanding. Likewise, believe in your thinking and ideas. Some people consider their thinking to be insignificant. They even consider the innovative thoughts arising from within them to be trivial, due to which they find themselves lagging behind in life. If this is your problem too, repeating the given self-suggestions will change your attitude towards yourself:

1. *"My imagination is beautiful, practical and impersonal, which will be beneficial for all, and that is why this imagination is soon becoming a reality."*
2. *"My decisions always turn out to be useful for me."*
3. *"I can stand up with pride and freedom."*
4. *"I believe my inner voice."*

To be healthy, learn to listen

Some people live in their own world all day long. They do not like to listen to others. Such people are likely to suffer from hearing problems. If noises trouble you or you have some problem in your ears, then along with medical help you can also restate this self-talk to speed up your recovery: *"I listen to the divine message. I listen to the sweet voices of everyone. I live together with people in harmony."*

Freedom from the fear of losing self-image

'What will people say? What will happen to my self-image?' If this is the fear preventing you from taking up new assignments, repeat the following self-dialogues as often as you can:

1. *"Now I have moved on far beyond the fear of people and disappointments. I am the creator of my life."*
2. *"Nature has given me the strength to overcome anything. I wish to experience everything without any worries. I am full of enthusiasm and energy."*

Take your own decisions; accept your parents as they are

Some children, even after maturing into adults, take all their decisions through their parents. They are not able to think for themselves or take their own decisions, due to which they do not develop fully or progress much in life. Such people spend their entire life blaming their parents. They can benefit from the following self-suggestions:

1. *"It is now safe for me to come out of my parents' shadow. I can now handle responsibilities happily because by taking up responsibilities I shall automatically be free."*

2. *"I forgive my father because whatever he did, he did so as per his understanding level and limitations he had at that time. He did not receive love from his parents. I forgive that unloved child."*

Freedom from the future

Worrying about the future leads to diseases of the eyes and blood pressure ailments. Diseases caused due to worries can be avoided by repeating this self-talk:

1. *"Miracles are happening in this world every day. I now accept the divine healing. I end my old self-talk and I allow the divine power, that operates the sun, moon and stars as per the divine plan, to work on me."*

2. *"Life is for me. I move ahead in life with faith and joy because I know that the best awaits me in the future."*

3. *"I believe in the way life works. That which takes care of each and every creature, even at the bottom of the sea, will take care of me too."*

Anger fuels ailments, guard against it

The fire of fury causes many ailments and rekindles old ones. This fact is known to all. Immediately after the eruption of anger, man feels a sense of unrest, burning sensation and distress. By being angry with others, man is unable to forgive them, and ends up harming himself. You would be doing yourself a big favor if you could forgive those who you do not wish to forgive. It will save you from imminent illnesses. To avoid illnesses caused by acidity, heart ailments and imbalance of the fire element in your body (*pitta*), reiterate the following self-dialogue:

1. *"I release my anger in a positive and creative manner. I appreciate myself for doing so."*
2. *"I am ready to forgive everyone."*
3. *"I believe in love. I like everybody."*

Sleep and self-talk

Every night before you sleep, repeat the following self-dialogue apart from your prayers: *"Lovingly I let go of this day and wish to go into a peaceful sleep because tomorrow will take care of itself."*

23

How To Benefit From A New Self-Affirmation Every Day

What we believe in, is our reality, i.e. it manifests in our world. We get prosperity or poverty, health or illness, joy or sorrow, good or bad, success or failure, respect or disrespect according to what we believe and have faith on. To turn your faith into bright, fresh and new, you need to recite positive self-affirmations and repeat them to yourself until your beliefs change for good.

How is your faith like? How much do you believe in the following statements?

1. Life does not want to see me prospering.
2. Good times don't last forever.
3. Success is hard to come by, I cannot win.
4. Nobody loves me.
5. I am not worthy of love.
6. I will meet with the same fate that my parents did.
7. I take a long time to learn, it is difficult to learn.
8. I am prone to illness.

9. I am born to suffer at the hands of others.

10. I am always vulnerable to the weather conditions.

11. Wealth doesn't stay with me for long.

12. Money does not come easily to me. That which comes, does not stay.

These wrong beliefs and misconceptions that man carries actually become true and manifest in his life. These beliefs and other such thoughts percolate into man through parents and teachers. Little children trust their parents and teachers and fully believe what they say. They hear from them things such as: 'People are there to deceive you… The world is bad… You are a boy and still you cry?… You are a girl, you are not supposed to do this…' There are so many such thoughts that children receive from them. These thoughts shape their life as they grow up. These thoughts decide the course of their life. If we want to live life happily and merrily, we must choose only those thoughts that provide us with the best possible life. Ask yourself about your problem, "Which kind of thoughts are responsible for my problem?" When you receive the answer, consciously change those thoughts with the help of self-talk. Always tell yourself, "I am ready for change."

A list of 31 self-affirmations, one for each day of the month, is given below. Recite these self-affirmations and repeat them to yourself throughout the day whenever possible. Pick the first self-affirmation on the first of every month and repeat it frequently all day long. Pick the second one on the second day of the month and work on it. Thus you can begin the day with a new self-affirmation every day. Doing so, at the end of the month you would have worked on 31 magical phrases. Within a few days, you will see the magic of self-talk working in your life.

Self-affirmations for each day

Day 1	:	"I have faith in supreme life, therefore fear and insecurity are merely thoughts that come and go. I am secure."
Day 2	:	"Every moment of life is special; at every stage of my life I love and accept myself."
Day 3	:	"Everybody is good and very friendly to me. I am always well-tuned with supreme life."
Day 4	:	"I am happy with what I am. I accept my body as it is, because my body is my friend."
Day 5	:	"Being successful is safe for me, Life loves me and therefore wants to see me successful."
Day 6	:	"I am easily releasing all that is not necessary for me now. It is right to cast aside all my false beliefs. The ailment that I do not need is leaving my body."
Day 7	:	"I am in harmony with life. I am not a victim of any guilt. I have forgiven myself."
Day 8	:	"I am God's property, only faith can touch me."

Day 9	:	"I express my feelings, expressing feelings is always safe for me."
Day 10	:	"My mind is not me. The mind is my tool; my tool is not me. My body is not me; the body is my friend."
Day 11	:	"I care for my experiences with love, joy and ease. There is magic in my hands and self-talk."
Day 12	:	"My heart dances to the tune of love along with everybody."
Day 13	:	"I speak politely and with love. I want to spread only happiness, knowledge and love."
Day 14	:	"I am magnificent. I never lose my splendour. I have given up worrying."
Day 15	:	"I am at the centre (heart) of life. Whatever I see, I accept it by being at that centre."
Day 16	:	"I am free of criticism. I have given up complaining and blaming. I easily adjust myself to change. My life enjoys divine guidance, therefore, I am always heading in the right direction."

Day 17	:	Love cures all ailments. I love everyone. I forgive everyone. Everyone forgives me. I am God's child."
Day 18	:	"I accept life entirely. I do not offer any resistance. I live life to its fullest with love."
Day 19	:	"I am complete; everything is done by me completely and on time."
Day 20	:	"I let go of my insistence and associated stress to be always right. I perform the right tasks at the right time with ease."
Day 21	:	"Nature has given me the strength to overcome anything. I wish to experience everything without any worries. I am full of enthusiasm and energy."
Day 22	:	"I am ready to transcend old boundaries and lead a new life. I am now freely expressing my qualities."
Day 23	:	"Adversities that don't terminate me make me tougher."
Day 24	:	"God cannot fall ill, therefore I too cannot fall ill."

Day 25 : "I am a part of God's creative opus. I therefore take part in creative and inventive ventures."

Day 26 : "I am enthusiastic and eager to change myself, to move ahead and build a new future."

Day 27 : "With every breath I am taking in the goodness of life and the grace of the Almighty that is being bestowed upon me."

Day 28 : "Only 'bright' deeds take place through me in my life. I receive only goodness from every experience."

Day 29 : "Miracles are taking place in this world every day. I now accept the divine healing. I am ending my old self-talk and allowing the divine power, that operates the sun, moon and stars as per the divine plan, to work on me."

Day 30 : "I believe in the way life works. That which takes care of everything, even the creatures at the bottom of the sea, will take care of me too.

Day 31 : "I am the Divine expression of God. I have understood how important and extraordinary I am."

■■■

Glossary

Word	Meaning
Tej/Bright	*Tej* is one of the most important words coined by Sirshree. 'Bright' is the closest translation of this word. Let us understand Bright or *Tej* with the help of an example. There is happiness and there is unhappiness. Here happiness means opposite of unhappiness. But there also exists happiness that is beyond both these polarities. It is the causeless, permanent, unremitting inner bliss. That is called *Tej* Happiness or Bright Happiness. This means that when the word '*Tej*' or 'Bright' is used as an adjective, then the word that is described as 'Bright' is beyond both polarities or beyond duality.
Tejguru	Spiritual master who guides you towards attainment of the final truth and stabilization in that truth.
Tej/Bright Truth	The Final Truth which is beyond truth and lies, it is the ultimate reality.

Truth	It refers to the ultimate truth, the supreme truth.
Tejgyan	Bright Knowledge – knowledge of the final truth which is beyond duality, beyond the grasp of the senses. If the knowledge is at the level of the body it means knowledge through the senses of hearing, seeing, touch and feeling. But that which is beyond duality, beyond the intellect, mind and body is *tejgyan*.
Bright Love	Supreme love or Bright love is unconditional, unquestioning, unlimited, unchanging, eternal, true love. It transcends love and hatred. It is overflowing love for the Lord and all His creations. All conditions cease in Bright Love, because love in itself is immense joy.
Bright friend	The friend who is beyond friendship or enmity. He is the enlightened one who understands your original nature and helps you reach your original nature. He helps you get over your delusions, false beliefs, mental patterns, fears and ignorance and always desires your well-being; even if you may sometimes feel otherwise.
Bright Silence/*Moun*	It signifies the state of inner silence which is the intrinsic nature of our true self. It is the state beyond sound and silence, beyond speech and thought. Words appear from this inner silence and also disappear in it. There is silence between every word and behind every word. There is silence between every thought and behind every thought. On the

paper of silence, the words of thought are written. To attain this silence is to attain Self.

Bright deeds	Deeds that are performed as a non-doer and create no bondage; liberated from *karma* (deeds and their results) and destiny.
Tejasthan	*Tejasthan* literally means the Bright Place. *Tejasthan* actually means that place where the Self is connected with the body; where the formless and the form unite; where the union (*yog*) takes place. It can be roughly considered to be in the area of the heart. At some places in the book, it has been loosely translated as the 'heart'. The second or external meaning of Tejasthan is a place where the knowledge of the truth is imparted.
Self	If written in capital in this book, i.e. 'Self', it implies the Universal Self, our true self, our original nature, Consciousness, Life, the Formless, the Witness, the Creator, God, Lord, Shiva, Allah…
Self-realization	Realizing who you are; realizing your true essence or your original nature.
Self-stabilization	Stabilizing in the experience of self-realization or constantly being in the Experience of the Self (or Experience of Being). This is what can be termed as the final liberation or *moksh*.
Self Expression	Expression of the true universal Self through the body. It also implies the expression of joy after self-realization in the form of service, creation, tears, devotional compositions, dance, etc.

Samadhi	The state of consciousness before time began. *Samadhi* is a state which cannot be adequately described in words; it can only be experienced. It can be said that *Samadhi* is being conscious of the true Self, transcending time and space. Or being in the state of undifferentiated beingness; a state of complete calm, tranquillity and joy but where the mind continues to be alert. (A second meaning is voluntarily entering the state of death, conscious death, arranged death, which is possible only with highly advanced saints and yogis. This second meaning has not been used in this book).
Service or *seva*	Serving others as if there is no other. Service can be in the form of physical efforts, wealth, sharing knowledge of the truth, etc.
Belief	False notion, assumption, something in which you believe but which is actually not true.
Contrast Mind	'Contrast mind' is a term used to distinguish between the two distinctive types of functioning of the mind. First is the intuitive mind, which is essential for our functioning. Second is the contrast mind which signifies that mind which compares and judges everything. It splits everything into two – white or black (good or bad), like the contrast control feature of the television. This is the mind which gives rise to fear, worry, envy, insecurity, deceit, assumptions, anger, lust, greed... It is present only in humans. It is the one which blocks us from seeing the

	Supreme Truth. But when it surrenders, it results in self-realization and unlimited, unremitting bliss.
Instinctive Mind	The instinctive or intuitive mind is the mind which performs every work instinctively with ease, and works to create the best according to its understanding. It is also responsible for the automatic working of all the organs of the body and the nervous system.

You can send your opinion or feedback on this book to :

Tej Gyan Foundation, Pimpri Colony, P. O. Box 25,
Pimpri, Pune – 411017 (Maharashtra), INDIA
email : mail@tejgyan.com

Write for Us

We welcome writers, translators and editors to join our team. If you would like to volunteer, please email us at: englishbooks@tejgyan.org or call : +91 90110 10963

About Sirshree

(Symbol of Acceptance)

Sirshree's spiritual quest which began during his childhood, led him on a journey through various schools of thought and meditation practices. His overpowering desire to attain the truth made him relinquish his teaching job. After a long period of contemplation, his spiritual quest culminated in the attainment of the ultimate truth. Sirshree says, **"All paths that lead to the truth begin differently, but end in the same way—with understanding. Understanding is the whole thing. Listening to this understanding is enough to attain the truth."**

Sirshree is the author of several spiritual books. His books have been translated in more than 10 languages and published by leading publishers such as Penguin and Hay House. He is the founder of Tej Gyan Foundation, a not-for-profit organization committed to raising mass consciousness by spreading "Happy Thoughts" with branches in the United States, India, Europe and Asia-Pacific. Sirshree's retreats have transformed the lives of thousands and his teachings have inspired various social initiatives for raising global consciousness.

His works include more than 100 books and 3000 discourses. Various luminaries and celebrities such as His Holiness the Dalai Lama, publishers Mr. Reid Tracy and Ms. Tami Simon and yoga master Dr. B. K. S Iyengar have released Sirshree's books and lauded his work. 'The Source' book series, authored by Sirshree, has sold more than 10 million copies in 5 years. His book *The Warrior's Mirror*, published by Penguin, was featured in the Limca Book of Records for being released on the same day in 11 languages.

Tejgyan... The Road Ahead
What is Tejgyan?

Tejgyan is the existential wisdom of the ultimate truth, which is beyond duality. In today's world, there are people who feel disharmony and are desperately trying to achieve balance in an unpredictable life. Tejgyan helps them in harmonizing with their true nature, the Self, thereby restoring balance in all aspects of their life.

And then there are those who are successful but feel a sense of emptiness or void within. Tejgyan provides them fulfillment and helps them to embark on a journey towards self-realization. There are others who feel lost and are seeking the meaning of life. Tejgyan helps them to realize the true purpose of human life.

All this is possible with Tejgyan due to a very simple reason. The experience of the ultimate truth is always available. The direct experience of this truth is possible provided the right method is known. Tejgyan is that method, that understanding. At Tej Gyan Foundation, Sirshree imparts this understanding through a System for Wisdom – a series of retreats that guides participants step by step

Magic of Ultimate Awakening Retreat

Magic of Ultimate Awakening is the flagship self-realization retreat offered by Tej Gyan Foundation The retreat is conducted in two languages – Hindi and English. The teachings of the retreat are non-denominational (secular).

This residential retreat is held for 3-5 days at the foundation's MaNaN Ashram amidst the glory of mountains and the pristine beauty of nature. This ashram is located at the outskirts of the city of Pune in India, and is well connected by air, road and rail. The retreat is also held at other centres of Tej Gyan Foundation across the world.

Participate in the *Magic of Ultimate Awakening* retreat to attain ageless wisdom through a unique simple 'System for Wisdom' so that you can:

1. Live from pure and still presence allowing the natural qualities of consciousness, viz. peace, love, joy, compassion, abundance and creativity to manifest.

2. Acquire simple tools to use in everyday life which help quieten the chattering mind, revealing your true nature.

3. Get practical techniques to access pure presence at will and connect to the source of all answers (the inner guru).

4. Discover missing links in practices of meditation *(dhyana)*, action *(karma)*, wisdom *(gyana)* and devotion *(bhakti)*.

5. Understand the nature of your body-mind mechanism to attain freedom from tendencies and patterns.

6. Learn practical methods to shift from mind-centred living to consciousness-centred living.

For retreats, contact +919921008060 or email: mail@tejgyan.com

A Mini retreat is also conducted, especially for teens (14-17 years) during summer and winter vacations

MaNaN Ashram

Survey No. 43, Sanas Nagar, Nandoshi gaon, Kirkatwadi Phata, Sinhagad Road, Dist. Pune 411024, Maharashtra, India.

About Tej Gyan Foundation

Tej Gyan Foundation (TGF) was established with the mission of creating a highly evolved society through all-round self development of every individual that transforms all the facets of his/her life. It is a non-profit organization founded on the teachings of Sirshree. The foundation has received the ISO certification (ISO 9001:2015) for its system of imparting wisdom. It has centres all across India as well as in other countries. The motto of Tej Gyan Foundation is 'Happy Thoughts'.

TGF is creating a highly evolved society through:

1. Tejgyan Programs (Retreats, Courses, Television and Radio Programs, Podcasts)

2. Tejgyan Products (Books, Tapes, Audio/Video CDs)

3. Tejgyan Projects (Value Education, Women Empowerment, Peace Initiatives)

TGF undertakes projects to elevate the level of consciousness among students, youth, women, senior citizens, teachers, doctors, leaders, organizations, police force, prisoners, etc.

Now you can register **online** for the following retreats

Maha Aasmani Param Gyan Shivir
(5 Days Residential Retreat in Hindi)

Magic of Ultimate Awakening Retreat
(3 Days Residential Retreat In English)

Mini Maha Aasmani Shivir
3 Days (Residential) Retreat for Teens

🔍 www.tejgyan.org

Books can be delivered at your doorstep by registered post or courier. You can request for the same through postal money order or pay by VPP. Please send the money order to any one of the following two addresses:

WOW Publishings Pvt. Ltd.

1. Registered Office: E-4, Vaibhav Nagar, Near Tapovan Mandir, Pimpri, Pune - 411017

2. Post Box No.36, Pimpri Colony Post Office, Pimpri, Pune - 411017

Phone No.: 9011013210 / 9623457873

You can also order your copy at the online store:
www.gethappythoughts.org

*Free Shipping plus 10% Discount on purchases above Rs. 300/-

For further details contact:

Tejgyan Global Foundation

Registered Office:

Happy Thoughts Building, Vikrant Complex, Near Tapovan Mandir, Pimpri, Pune 411017, Maharashtra, India.
Contact No: 020-27411240, 27412576
Email: mail@tejgyan.com

MaNaN Ashram:

Survey No. 43, Sanas Nagar, Nandoshi gaon, Kirkatwadi Phata, Sinhagad Road, Tal. Haveli, Dist. Pune 411024, Maharashtra, India.

Contact No: 992100 8060.

Hyderabad: 9885558100, **Bangalore:** 9880412588,
Delhi : 9891059875, **Nashik:** 9326967980, **Mumbai:** 9373440985

For accessing our unique 'System for Wisdom' from self-help to self-realization, please follow us on:

happy thoughts The Tej Gyan	Website	www.tejgyan.org
YouTube	Video Channel	www.youtube.com/tejgyan For Q&A videos: http://goo.gl/YA81DQ
facebook	Social networking	www.facebook.com/tejgyan
twitter	Social networking	www.twitter.com/sirshree
Internet Radio icon	Internet Radio	http://www.tejgyan.org/internetradio.aspx

Online Shopping
www.gethappythoughts.org

Pray for World Peace along with thousands of others
at 09:09 a.m. and p.m. every day

www.ingramcontent.com/pod-product-compliance
Lightning Source LLC
LaVergne TN
LVHW091048100526
838202LV00077B/3079